•••••••••••••••••••••••••••••••••

MEG
AND THE
MYSTERY OF THE
BLACK-MAGIC
CAVE

•••••••••••••••••••••••••••••••••

*MEG
AND THE
MYSTERY OF THE
BLACK-MAGIC
CAVE*

ABOUT THIS BOOK

Merrybones, Maine. . . . Even the name of the place sounded mysterious and exciting. Meg Duncan had traveled a great deal in her young life, but she had never before visited the north woods of Maine. Uncle Hal owned a cabin in the woods and sometimes went there to fish and relax. But this time, he was going for a different reason—to help a friend in need. How did this town get its unusual name? Meg wondered. And what was the "frightful problem" that Uncle Hal's friend, Emily Hawthorne, had mentioned in her letter?

Meg and Kerry soon discovered that Merrybones got its name from the strange happenings around Wigwam Cave. Indian witch doctors had used the cave once. There had supposedly been other witches there, too. Some people still said that when the night was right and the moon was full, the witches might come again . . . thirteen terrible witches, who could cast an evil spell on anyone who dared try to solve THE MYSTERY OF THE BLACK-MAGIC CAVE.

Meg

AND THE MYSTERY OF
THE BLACK-MAGIC CAVE

by Holly Beth Walker

illustrated by Cliff Schule
cover illustration by Olindo Giacomini

GOLDEN PRESS
Western Publishing Company, Inc.
Racine, Wisconsin

CONTENTS

1
WELCOME TO MERRYBONES

"Check your seat belts, girls. We'll be landing in a few minutes."

Meg Duncan's uncle had to shout above the roar of his small yellow airplane. Turning in the cockpit, he looked back at his two young passengers—brown-eyed Meg and her friend Kerry Carmody.

For most of the day, the girls had been in the plane, flying over mountains and lakes and cities. The drone of the engine had almost lulled them to sleep, but now they came instantly to life. They sat up, eagerly scanning the dark woods below.

"Are we getting close to Merrybones, Uncle Hal?" asked Meg, pushing back her thick, dark braids.

"Right over there, Meg." The young man, whose name was Harold Ashley, pointed toward a clearing at the edge of the lake. "For my money, it's the nicest town in Maine. You and Kerry should have a grand time spending your vacation up here.''

"I see the church steeple!'' Kerry cried suddenly. She was closest to the window, her pert freckled face alight with anticipation. "And that looks like a hotel —there on the hill!''

Meg had spotted the buildings, too, and her heart beat faster. *Merrybones, Maine.* . . . Even the name of the place sounded mysterious and exciting, she thought.

Meg Duncan had traveled a great deal in her young life. Her father worked for the government, and when she was a very little girl—before her lovely mother died—she had even lived for a time in the Orient. But she had never before visited the north woods of Maine.

Uncle Hal had talked often about this hidden village below. He owned a cabin in the woods and sometimes went there to fish and relax. Now Meg could hardly wait for the plane to land so she and Kerry could start exploring for themselves.

Kerry was Meg's dearest friend. The two girls lived around the corner from each other, in the small Virginia city of Hidden Springs. They were about the same age and had wonderful fun together, but they were almost exact opposites.

Lovable Kerry, with her flyaway blond hair and

14

blue eyes, was apt to be impulsive. She was quick to laugh and quick to cry—and sometimes quick to jump into hot water without thinking. That wasn't surprising. The Carmody family had seven children and twice as many pets, and Kerry often had to jump fast just to keep up.

Meg was dark in coloring, with large eyes and soft, olive-tinted skin. Due to her constant association with adults, her reactions were cooler and more thoughtful than Kerry's. She was alone in the world, except for her father and, of course, her beloved Uncle Hal. He was still a bachelor and somewhat like a big brother to her. Unfortunately, Hal lived and worked in Washington, D.C., and Meg's father was often away on business. So Meg's home was a quiet one.

When she wasn't with Kerry, Meg was usually deep in a book or practicing her ballet. Sometimes she helped Mrs. Wilson, her father's housekeeper. She loved to polish the heavy old silver that had belonged to her mother.

Meg had just one pet, a beautiful Siamese cat named Thunder. Kerry called him "The Untouchable," because he would go only to Meg.

One thing the girls did have in common was their devotion to mystery and adventure. More than once, back in Hidden Springs, they had helped to solve a knotty problem for someone in trouble. It was, in fact, a small mystery that had brought them on this trip to the north woods.

Uncle Hal hadn't planned to come to Maine this summer, Meg recalled. He had been all packed to go to Hawaii. Then he received a strange letter from Merrybones.

It was from Emily Hawthorne, a young Merrybones schoolteacher. It wasn't what her letter said that worried Uncle Hal; it was what it *didn't* say.

"I hope you are coming to Merrybones soon," the young woman had written. "I have a frightful problem and need your advice. I dare not discuss it on the phone." The letter had an ominous sound, and Uncle Hal had changed his plans at once.

"Who could fail a damsel in distress?" he had explained to Meg. "If I can help a friend in any way, I want to do it."

Then, to Meg's great delight, he had invited her and Kerry to go with him. School had been out for several weeks, and the girls had been hungry for excitement.

"I'll take you along on two conditions," he had said. "First, you'll have to get your parents' permission." (There had been no problem about *that*.)

"And second, you'll please try to keep your pretty little noses out of things in Merrybones that don't concern you.

"After I've helped Emily—if that's possible," he added, "I intend to enjoy myself. I'm going to fish a little, paint a little, and loaf a lot. If you two get into any awkward predicaments up there, don't come to me."

"We'll be good," Meg had promised, laughing. She wasn't worried; she knew no one would come running faster than Uncle Hal if she and Kerry needed help.

Not that they were likely to get into any trouble in a dead-end place like the town below, Meg thought as she checked her belt.

The plane was directly over the town now. She stared ruefully down at a cluster of unadorned, squarish buildings. Merrybones was supposed to date from Colonial times, and it looked as though it hadn't changed since!

"Your town doesn't look very *merry* to me, Uncle Hal," Meg called out. "I don't see a single, solitary person."

Her uncle laughed. "Don't be misled, Maggie-me-love," he shouted back. "It's suppertime up here. God-fearing folks are inside eating their 'vittles.' I'm

17

sure at least a hundred good souls live around Merry-bones—including the dogs—and that's not counting the summer folks who come to fish and hike."

"I just hope there are some horses!" That was Kerry, yelling in Meg's ear.

Meg had to grin at that. Kerry wouldn't want to go to heaven if there were no horses there to ride!

The plane was nosing downward now, rushing toward a narrow runway hacked from the edge of the pine forest. Kerry held her breath and clutched Meg's arm. They made a neat landing and rolled along the rough ground to the end of the runway; then Uncle Hal turned the plane around and taxied back to a sheet metal hangar.

Meg saw that there were other small planes parked nearby. One was painted white and had a red cross on the side.

"That one belongs to Fred Willoughby," Uncle Hal remarked as he unfastened his seat belt and un-latched the door. "He's the only doctor in this neck of the woods. He and his nurse are apt to fly off at any hour of the day or night to answer a distress call."

A tall, lean-faced man came from the hangar as Uncle Hal jumped to the ground.

"How do, Mr. Ashley," he said. "I saw you comin' in and went to phone Mrs. Stoner. Her boy, Clyde,

will drive out in his jeep to get you."

"Thank you, Mr. Link."

When Hal turned back to help Meg and Kerry from the plane, he found the eager pair already at his side. They were dressed exactly alike, except for color. Kerry's jeans and sweater were the same bright blue as her eyes. Meg wore red.

It wasn't long till the jeep came bouncing toward them across the field. It was driven by a dark-haired boy of about sixteen. He greeted Meg's uncle with a grin and a handshake. He stared rather shyly at the girls.

"My sister, Betsy, will be glad to have you staying with us," he said politely when he was introduced.

"You'll be seeing a lot of Clyde and his sister for the next two weeks," said Uncle Hal. "The Stoners own the big house near my place. I've arranged for you to room there."

It didn't take long to stow the luggage in the back of the jeep. Then, with a wave to Mr. Link, Uncle Hal jumped in beside the driver. The girls, in the backseat, had to park their feet atop the suitcases.

"Isn't the air wonderful, Kerry?" said Meg as they sped toward town. She took a deep, deep breath. The smell of lake water and pine trees filled her with excitement.

"Oh, look!" cried Kerry suddenly. "There's a deer!"

Meg turned just in time. A graceful fawn was darting into the woods, looking almost rosy in the evening light.

"We've already had our supper," Clyde Stoner was telling Uncle Hal, "but Ma put the kettle on again, soon as she heard you were landing. Said she'd have a hot meal for all of you by the time you're ready."

"We'll be ready," Uncle Hal delcared. "We had only tuna sandwiches for lunch on the plane. You can drop us at my fishing shack, Clyde," he added. "I'll leave my gear there, and we'll walk down to the big house in a few minutes. I can't wait to show Meg and Kerry my hideaway in the woods."

And they could hardly wait to see it. Meg had a curious feeling that she and Kerry were rushing headlong into a new and exciting adventure.

2
THE SIGN OF
THIRTEEN

Uncle Hal's hideaway was more than a shack. It looked quite small, nestled among giant trees on a hill, but Meg found its single room comfortable and spacious.

The walls were lined with golden knotty pine. There were a cot and a table, and several easy chairs were placed invitingly in front of the stone fireplace.

Meg spied an unfinished oil painting on an easel in front of the north window. It was of an old house near a lake. She liked to dabble in painting, too, so she ran to study her uncle's work.

"It's very good, Uncle Hal," she said slowly, "but it's not a bit like you. You've always loved color, and this is all grays and blacks—"

"That's the Stoner house, Meg." Her uncle came to stand behind her. "It's sturdy and plain, like the folks around here. The family had money years ago, when the sawmills were working near here. Now Mrs. Stoner is a widow, and they take in boarders for a living."

"What is this, Mr. Ashley?"

Kerry had been busily poking around behind them and had discovered some odd rocks on the mantel. She stood near Meg now, twisting one of them in her hands and staring down at it curiously.

Meg and her uncle turned. The young man frowned thoughtfully.

"I'm not sure what that is, Kerry," he said. He took the object from her and held it out for his niece to see. "What do you make of it, Meg?"

Meg's shining dark braids fell forward as she bent to study the stone. It was small and gray. One side was smooth, but when she turned it over, she saw the odd carvings—circles and triangles, all drawn around a starlike form.

"Could it be a rune stone, Uncle Hal?" Meg asked, looking up. "The Vikings came to this land about a thousand years ago. They wrote on stones—"

Her uncle smiled. "That's a very good guess, Meg. It's exactly what I hoped when I first spied these things."

Meg's uncle worked for a museum, and he was always on the lookout for ancient things to add to his collections. But now he shook his head. "These carvings weren't done by the Vikings," he said regretfully. "They aren't even very old, Meg; I'm sure they were done with a modern electric tool. I picked the rocks up in the woods, near a place called Wigwam Cave.

"The question is," he went on, with a puzzled expression, "why anybody would want to carve black-magic signs on rocks in the backwoods of Maine."

"Black Magic?" Meg's dark eyes widened. At the same instant, she heard a startled gasp from Kerry.

Uncle Hal nodded. "Just such symbols were used in witchcraft back in the middle ages," he explained. "They were used to create magic spells. This five-pointed figure is called a pentacle. It's a great favorite of witches."

He took the small rock from Meg. "When the pentacle sign points up, like this," he said, "it supposedly means good luck. But when it points *down,* that's a bad omen. Somebody had better watch out!"

Kerry laughed nervously. "But there aren't any witches today," she protested, "except at Halloween parties."

"Don't be so sure, Kerry." Uncle Hal put the rock down on the coffee table. "The so-called art of black magic is still practiced among primitive tribes—and among some foolish people in our own country, I'm afraid.''

He turned then, smiling at the two sober young faces. "However, I doubt that we need to worry about witches around Merrybones," he said lightly. "Right now, I'm more curious about what is bubbling in Mrs. Stoner's kettle at the big house. What do you say, girls? Shall we have our dinner?''

The cabin had no electricity, so Uncle Hal had lighted a battery-powered lantern when they first arrived. Now he picked it up to take with them.

Just then there was a knock at the door.

"I wonder who that is," said Meg.

"Only one way to find out." Uncle Hal strode to the door and pulled it open. Meg and Kerry stared past him.

A slender young woman stood on the step outside. She wore a neat gray suit. Her pale yellow hair, gleaming softly in the lamplight, framed a troubled face. Without being told, Meg knew who she was.

"Why, Emily—do come in." Uncle Hal may have been a bit surprised, but he smiled warmly at his visitor. "News travels fast," he said. "We just flew in a few minutes ago.''

"I know." The young woman stepped past him. "I stopped by the big house. Clyde Stoner said you and the girls were here. Please forgive me, Hal, for bothering you so soon," she added swiftly. "I know you must be tired, but I just couldn't wait to talk to you."

Kerry nudged Meg's arm. "Isn't she pretty?" she whispered.

Meg nodded, but she couldn't take her eyes from the newcomer. She really was beautiful, except for that haunted look in her eyes.

"No bother at all," Uncle Hal said in his gentle way. He led the girl to one of the big chairs. "I intended to call on you this evening.

"This is my niece, Margaret Duncan," he went on, "and her friend Kerry Carmody. They came along for the ride. Miss Emily Hawthorne, girls."

"H-Hello." Emily turned unseeing eyes toward the girls. She made a weak effort to smile.

At that, Meg took Kerry's arm and urged her toward the door. "We'll look around outside, Uncle Hal—"

The young woman stopped them. "No, please, Meg. I want you to stay. Your uncle has told me how clever you two are at solving mysteries. I'd like you to hear my story."

Meg and Kerry came slowly back, as puzzled by the girl's behavior as Uncle Hal plainly was.

He leaned against the mantel now, smiling down

at the seated guest. "Your letter hinted at some dark problem, Emily," he said. "I flew up as soon as I could. How can we help you?"

"I'm not sure that you can," the girl said in a weary voice. Then she opened her purse and drew out two envelopes. She handed one of them to Hal. "Someone has been sending me threatening letters. I can't understand why.

"That's the earliest one, Hal. You can see that it was mailed from Boston. I thought it was a joke."

Uncle Hal opened the letter and read it. Without a word, he handed it on to Meg.

With Kerry looking over her shoulder, Meg glanced down at the paper. The words were in crude verse:

> TEACHER, TEACHER, KEEP YOUR COOL;
> DON'T TELL STORIES OUT OF SCHOOL.
> PACK YOUR BOOKS AND FLY AWAY—
> IF YOU DON'T, YOU'LL RUE THE DAY.

The message was unsigned. But at the bottom of the page was something Meg had seen only moments before. A five-pointed figure had been crudely sketched in black ink. Within it was printed the number thirteen.

Meg felt an icy tingle at the nape of her neck. This was the same sign that was engraved on the gray rocks. *The magic pentacle.* Could there be any connection? She was careful not to glance at the coffee table.

"The writing is in plain block letters," she said thoughtfully. "It wouldn't be easy to identify the writer."

"And it's on plain old school notepaper," put in Kerry. Her small pixy face was unusually serious. "Maybe one of your pupils is playing a joke, Miss Hawthorne."

The young teacher shook her head. "I suspected that at first, Kerry. Some of the bigger boys like to tease me. I felt sure Kent Wiley had sent that letter while he was away on vacation. But then the second letter came, and Kent had been home for days. And soon after that, Melissa disappeared. I know Kent wouldn't resort to—to. . . ."

Uncle Hal had been studying the second letter. Now he handed it to Meg. The smile was gone from his face.

Meg found this one much like the first but even more puzzling.

> TEACHER, TEACHER, LISTEN WELL;
> ONLY YOU CAN BREAK THIS SPELL.
> WITCHES HAVE MELISSA HEXED—
> LEAVE AT ONCE, OR YOU ARE NEXT.

This message, too, bore the black-magic sign.

"Who is Melissa?" asked Meg, looking up.

"My cat," the young woman answered. "She's a big animal—coal black, with green eyes. I've had her since she was a kitten, when I lived in California. She's been missing for a week, and I've searched everywhere. . . . I'm so confused," she added. "I have no idea who's doing this to me, or why."

Uncle Hal reached out a hand and drew Emily to her feet. There was concern in his face, but his voice was reassuring. "The letters might still be a practical joke, Emily," he insisted. "As for your cat . . . she may have wandered off in the woods—"

"No." There were sudden tears in Emily's eyes. "Melissa never wandered far from the house, and she always wore a little green collar with a bell. The night she disappeared, I found that same five-pointed star drawn on my front door—and *this* was hanging on the knob.''

She pulled the green collar from her purse. A tiny silver bell tinkled forlornly.

Meg felt the sting of tears in her own eyes. She knew how crushed she would be if anything happened to her cat, Thunder.

Kerry was outraged. ''That's the meanest thing in the world,'' she declared, ''stealing your pet! Meg and I will do everything we can to help you find Melissa.''

Even Uncle Hal looked grim by now. ''The important thing,'' he said flatly, ''is to find out who took the cat—and who sent Emily these poisonous letters.'' He took them from Meg and studied them again with narrowed eyes. ''Do you know anyone in Boston, Emily?''

The young woman shook her head. ''As you know, Hal, I've lived most of my life with an aunt on the West Coast. Of course, I was born right here in this town, but I left when I was only five.''

''Why did you come back?'' asked Kerry curiously.

''I came here on my vacation last summer. I wanted to find out something about my family—how my father had died. I found out that the town needed a

31

teacher for the upper grades, so I decided to stay.''

Her lips began to tremble. "I—I admire the people around here, but they aren't very friendly to outsiders. Even though I was born here, I'm an outsider. Someone is trying to drive me away, and I don't know who it is or what I've done that they don't want me to do.''

"You've done nothing at all," Meg's uncle said firmly. He put the letters into his pocket. "We'll talk about this later. Right now, Emily, you're going down to the big house with us, for a cup of tea. I'm sure Mrs. Stoner will be happy to have you.''

He turned to Meg and Kerry. "Keep your lips sealed and your eyes and ears wide open," he suggested. "Somebody around here is playing a cruel and thoughtless prank. I want to know why.''

It was quite dark when they stepped out of the cabin and started down the path toward the Stoner house. Kerry pressed close to Meg's side. "Did you notice that those black-magic signs on the letters pointed *down?*" she whispered.

Meg nodded, but she made no reply. She was thinking of something even more startling. Both pentacles enclosed the number thirteen.

In stories she had read, witches most often gathered in *groups of thirteen*.

3
BELLIGERENT BETSY

"Welcome back, Mr. Ashley."

Mrs. Stoner met Uncle Hal and his companions at the door of the big gray house. She was a tall, angular woman, in an immaculate white apron. Meg noticed a certain coolness in her attitude toward Emily, but it was plain that she was easy prey for Uncle Hal's charm. "Come right in," she invited warmly.

After the travelers had washed up, Mrs. Stoner led them to an enormous old-fashioned kitchen. "I thought it would be cozier for you to eat in here, Mr. Ashley," she said as they sat down at the table. "My other boarders finished eating long ago."

The kitchen had a modern stove and refrigerator, but an old brick fireplace remained—complete with warming ovens and shining copper pans. A small fire burned on the hearth.

"Just leftovers," Mrs. Stoner said crisply. She

plunked a big platter of steaming food down in front of Uncle Hal. Then, at his request, she brewed some tea for Emily.

Clyde Stoner was nowhere to be seen, but his sister, Betsy, helped her mother serve. She was a year or two older than Meg and Kerry and looked like her mother. She had the same bony face and mousy brown hair. *She* didn't smile at *all*.

Kerry punched Meg in the ribs. "Betsy's brother said she'd be so-o-o happy to have us," she hissed. "She looks as if she'd like to bite us."

"Shhhh!" Meg shook her head warningly, but she had to agree. Betsy Stoner was definitely sulky and unfriendly.

The supper may have been "just leftovers," but it was delicious. Uncle Hal chatted lightly with Emily during the meal, but Meg and Kerry were too busy eating to talk much. They had boiled beef and fresh vegetables and a sweet corn bread called johnnycake. Dessert was blueberries with clotted cream.

"Mmmmmmmm!" Uncle Hal beamed at sight of the luscious fruit. "The pride of Maine. How lucky can a mortal be, Meg—to arrive just at blueberry time!"

For the first time, Meg saw Emily Hawthorne smile. It was a lovely sight.

34

"Oh, I do hope you'll stay for the blueberry social, Hal," she said. "The Blueberry Bash, the kids call it. I wasn't here in time last summer, but they tell me it's held every year at the schoolhouse—for the library fund. Each housewife makes up her finest blueberry recipe, and for the price of one small ticket, you can stuff yourself royally."

"That's right," said Mrs. Stoner, with an air of pride. She glanced at her daughter. "Fact is," she added, "Betsy is going up around Wigwam Cave tomorrow to gather berries for me to cook up. There's lots of them now on Blueberry Ridge."

Meg looked at Kerry. *Wigwam Cave!* Wasn't that where Uncle Hal found those strange rocks with the black-magic signs?

It was Kerry who spoke. "Could we go along?" she asked eagerly. "I've never picked wild blueberries in my life."

"Why, of course," Mrs. Stoner answered at once. "Betsy'll be happy to have you. Won't you, Betsy?"

Betsy didn't look happy at all. But she nodded her head grudgingly.

"You can show the girls their room now, Betsy," Mrs. Stoner said. "I'm afraid it's kind of small, Meg. We were about full up when your uncle called to say you were coming with him."

35

"I'm sure it will be just fine," said Meg graciously. She jumped to her feet, smiling at Uncle Hal and Emily. Then she and Kerry followed the reluctant Betsy up two flights of stairs to the room.

It *was* small. Meg realized at once that it had been created out of part of the attic, but she immediately fell in love with it. The ceiling slanted almost to the floor, and the walls were covered with quaint yellow paper. The room was furnished with braided rugs and odds and ends of Colonial furniture.

"There's your suitcases. Clyde brought them up when he came from the plane." Betsy, about to leave, was speaking to them for the first time. "The bathroom's on the second floor," she snapped. "And if you want a hot breakfast in the morning, you better get up early. If you don't, it's cornflakes and milk."

She closed the door with a bang.

Meg grinned at Kerry, amused in spite of her irritation at Betsy's outrageous behavior.

"What do you suppose is the matter with *her?*" Kerry demanded.

"I don't know, but I'm beginning to suspect that Emily Hawthorne was right about the people of Merrybones. Some of them don't seem to like outsiders."

Kerry was opening her suitcase. She hung a yellow

36

Sunday dress in the wardrobe. "They seem to like your uncle," she said.

Meg's dark eyes grew soft. "Who could help loving Uncle Hal?" she answered warmly.

It was Kerry who, later that evening, uncovered the secret of Betsy's bad humor.

The girls had taken baths and were in their pajamas; the ever-curious Kerry was exploring the room. She had already tried a locked door that led to the other part of the attic. Failing that, she lifted the lid of an old chest at the foot of the bed. Inside she found the neatly stored keepsakes of a small girl.

She pulled forth a rag doll. It had yellow braids and button eyes. "This must be Betsy's own room!" Kerry exclaimed. "See, Meg—there's her snapshot on the mirror. And here's one of her old dolls."

Meg glanced around. "Put it back, Kerry," she ordered. "We mustn't snoop in her things."

Meg was standing near the open window. She had been watching her uncle escort Emily back toward the village. Now, as she started to turn from the window, something drew her attention to the cabin on the hill.

She thought she saw a flash of light. Then a shadow seemed to break from the cabin and melt into the

37

dark woods. It could have been an animal. . . .

A moment later, Meg wasn't sure she had seen anything at all, but her heart was beating fast, and the enormous pine trees made her think of brooding hags. *Witches have Melissa hexed/Leave at once, or you are next.*

What *had* happened to Melissa? All at once Meg felt icy cold. She pulled down the window and ran to crawl into the warm bed. Kerry was already snuggling down.

Meg was more tired than she knew. She had barely closed her eyes—or so it seemed—when she heard a sharp rapping at the door. She awoke to find it was morning.

The door opened a crack, and Betsy stuck her homely little face inside. She didn't look quite as cross as she had the night before. On the other hand, neither was she smiling.

Meg sat up and sent her most winning smile over to Betsy. "We took your room," she said apologetically. "I'm so sorry, Betsy. I don't blame you for being mad; it's a darling room."

The other girl turned quite pink. Then a shy smile lit her face, and she didn't look nearly so plain.

"I *was* mad last night," she admitted. "Ma made me sleep on the daybed in her room. It's got springs

38

that stick into you. But I don't mind now, really. Ma sent me to fetch you for breakfast.''

By now Kerry was awake, and soon all three were talking and laughing together like old friends.

Breakfast was served in the dining room that morning, so the girls got to meet the other boarders.

There was one young couple—the Millards—with a four-year-old girl. There were several well-dressed women on vacation and one old man who had come to Maine to fish. He sat by himself at the end of the table and devoured a mountain of pancakes and countless sausages.

Just as they finished eating, Uncle Hal came down from the cabin. He called Meg and Kerry into the hall.

''Did you learn any more about those letters, Uncle Hal?'' Meg asked anxiously.

He shook his dark head. ''I'm afraid Emily told us all she knows. But you could see that she's badly frightened. She doesn't know whom to trust around here.''

''I don't blame her,'' said Kerry. ''Somebody has already taken her cat, and if she doesn't go away as they want her to, something bad might happen to *her*.''

The young man looked grim. ''We have to make

sure that it doesn't, Kerry. The poison-pen letters might be impossible to trace, but if we can find out *why* they were mailed to Emily, that mysterious 'somebody' you mention might be exposed.''

He turned to Meg. "I'm going to poke around a bit this morning and ask a few cautious questions. I want to talk with Officer Sykes. He's the local policeman and also operates the riding stables in his spare time. I'm pretty sure Sykes was living here when Emily was a little girl. He might be able to give us a clue.''

"Do you want us to do anything?'' asked Meg.

"Not just now, honey. We don't want the guilty party to suspect that we're here to help Emily. You and Kerry go berry picking with Betsy, just as you planned.''

He gave her a loving hug. "It's beautiful up around Wigwam Cave,'' he added. "You should have a wonderful time. I'll see you when you get back.''

4

AT WIGWAM CAVE

In spite of her concern for Uncle Hal's friend, Meg couldn't help feeling lighthearted as she set off with Betsy and Kerry for Blueberry Ridge.

Each girl carried a berry basket. Two were empty, and one was filled with a generous lunch of sandwiches and lemonade.

It was a golden day. Sunlight spangled the forest trail, and a pleasant breeze blew through the evergreens. Now that she knew Meg and Kerry, Betsy was friendly and talkative. To Meg's delight, she named the strange birds and flowers as they went along.

Before they reached the ridge, they had to cross a shallow stream. There was a bridge nearby, but, true to their shared spirit of adventure, they took off their sneakers and waded across.

The blueberries—millions and millions of them—

grew on a rocky hillside, close to the ground. The girls went immediately to work, picking the fruit and filling the two empty baskets. They ate as they picked, of course, and soon their lips and tongues were as blue as the berries themselves.

"That's enough, I guess," said Betsy at last. She plumped herself down on a rock. "If Ma wants more berries, we can always come again. The Blueberry Bash isn't for ten days, anyway. She'll put these in the freezer and then make deep-dish pies."

"Sounds yummy," declared Meg. Then she could wait no longer to ask her question. "Where is that place called Wigwam Cave, Betsy? Your mother said it was near here."

"The other side of the hill," answered Betsy. "We can eat our lunch there if you want." She got to her feet and picked up the basket with their lunch. "Come on."

The strange rock formation really did look like an Indian wigwam. Great wedges of granite had fallen from the mountains in prehistoric times. Like gigantic jackstraws, they landed partly upright, leaning against each other and forming a triangular opening.

"There's a real cave inside," said Betsy. "Come on; I'll show you."

43

She led Meg and Kerry toward the jagged doorway. Beyond it was a large open room, with a hole in the roof where the rocks did not quite wedge together.

Just inside the door, Betsy came to a sudden halt. "Be quiet!" she whispered. But Kerry, at her side, couldn't hold back a cry of surprise.

"Look, Meg!"

Then Meg saw it, too. A candle was sputtering on a flat rock at the far end of the cave, casting eerie tongues of light across the rock walls.

The three girls looked warily around the shadowy cave. Betsy even crept toward a jumble of boulders at one side and peered behind them. There was nobody there.

Then Meg noticed something on the floor, and her heart skipped a beat. Scratched in the soft, moist earth was another pentacle! It was pointed toward the burning candle. Inside the magic figure were prints of small human feet and the paw prints of an animal.

With Kerry at her side, Meg walked carefully around the pentacle and stared down at the candle. It was black and almost burned out. There were the remains of several others like it on the flat rock. Beside the candle lay two small stones etched with familiar symbols.

"Like the rocks in the cabin!" Kerry gasped.

Meg pressed her arm warningly, then turned to face Betsy. "Who do you think lit those candles?"

"I don't know any more than you," Betsy retorted, "but a lot of funny things happen up around here. Some folks are afraid of this place.

"The Indians had a legend about it. They thought these smooth gray rocks were the bones of a giant, and when the witch doctor made his spells, the bones jumped up and down. They called them dancing bones."

"Dancing bones—Merrybones." Meg managed to

45

laugh a little. "Maybe that's where your town gets its name."

"I guess so," said Betsy solemnly. "Maybe an earthquake made the bones jump."

Meg was looking down. At that instant, a shadow moved across the triangle of sunlight on the floor. Meg looked up quickly at the cave entrance.

Someone was standing there.

It was a little girl of seven or eight. She had a small, thin face beneath a cap of short, black hair. Her feet were bare, and she was dressed in a long white thing that looked like an old lace curtain.

And in her arms was a huge black cat with gleaming green eyes!

For a moment the three girls in the cave were spellbound. When they could move, the vision was gone.

Betsy dashed toward the opening, followed by Meg and Kerry.

Girl and cat had slipped away among the trees, but Kerry caught a glimpse of white. "Let's follow her," she shouted. "That could be Melissa!"

Off they went, running and stumbling through the underbrush. They saw her again down at the river. She splashed across in her bare feet. Having their shoes on, they had to race downstream to the bridge.

"She's going toward the old lumber mill," Betsy said, panting. "It's around that hill."

The child had disappeared by now, and when the three rounded the hill, she was still nowhere to be seen.

Meg stopped and stared. The old lumber mill loomed before them. It had been long abandoned. The machinery was rusty; the sheds had fallen into ruin.

"She's hiding, I bet," declared Betsy.

They prowled about for a little while. Once Meg thought she heard the whine of the cat. She stopped and listened, but it didn't come again.

"Do you know who that little girl is?" Meg asked Betsy as they all started back to the cave, where they had left the baskets of berries and their lunch.

"Yes," said Betsy. "That's Lisa—Lisa McKay, I think. She's just been here a few days. She's visiting her aunt at the old Hawthorne place."

Meg looked quickly around. "Does it belong to Emily Hawthorne?" she asked. "I thought she lived near the school."

"She does," said Betsy. She reached out and pulled a spray of juniper from a tree and sniffed it. "The house used to belong to her family, years ago, and people just kept calling it the Hawthorne place.

"Miss Bell lives there now. She's a schoolteacher, too. She teaches the little kids, and she's so strict, all of them are scared to death of her."

"I wonder if it was Lisa who lit that black candle," said Meg thoughtfully as they came in sight of Wigwam Cave once more.

"And I wonder what she was doing in that silly old lace thing," put in Kerry. "I guess she was playing make-believe."

"Well, I don't care." Betsy sounded impatient. "I'm starving. You left our lunch inside there, Kerry. You go and get it."

Kerry looked toward the cave so unhappily that Meg went inside and brought out the basket.

"Let's eat down by the river," she suggested. "This place is too spooky."

5

A CLUE FROM THE PAST

Both Meg and Kerry were tired when they returned to the Stoner house, but they felt better after they had cleaned up and changed into fresh clothes. Then they hurried up to the cabin to report to Uncle Hal.

Uncle Hal had a visitor—the local doctor. He was a big handsome man who didn't seem too much older than Uncle Hal himself, but he was already gray at the temples, and there were lines of worry around his kindly brown eyes. He was sitting in one of the easy chairs, smoking a pipe.

"Dr. Willoughby and I have been out on the lake fishing," Uncle Hal said with a smile. "Emily's coming down, and we're going to cook supper for you girls. Meg, you can make one of your famous salads.

"The girls have been up near Wigwam Cave picking blueberries," he added, turning back to his guest.

At mention of the cave, a peculiar expression came over the doctor's face. "I wouldn't advise you young ladies to go up there by yourselves," he said somewhat sternly. "There have been accidents around those rocks. Not long ago—"

At that moment there was an urgent call from outside. "Doctor—Dr. Willoughby! Are you there?"

He stood up at once. There was a weary look on his face. "That's my nurse, Della Armstrong, Hal," he said. "One of the Wiley children is seriously sick. We may have to fly him out to a hospital."

"I'm sorry to hear that," said Hal. He opened the door, and Nurse Armstrong came striding in.

Meg and Kerry stared at her with interest. She was far from young, but she was dressed in a sensible khaki-colored pants suit. Her face, under gray, short hair, was strong and weather-beaten, and her eyes gleamed with pent-up energy.

Meg noticed dried scratches on her hands and arms. She looked, Meg thought, as if she could, and would, brave jungles or climb mountains to aid the sick.

"The Wiley boy came down to the office, Doctor," she said in clipped tones. "The baby's worse. Mrs. Wiley wants you right away."

"Thank you, Nurse." The doctor held out his hand

to Hal. "No fish fry now," he said resignedly. "At least I had the fun of catching them."

As the men said good-bye, Meg saw Nurse Armstrong glance curiously around the room. She seemed interested in the cabin and everything in it.

Dr. Willoughby spoke to the girls as he left. "I hope you'll enjoy your stay in Merrybones, Meg and Kerry," he said. "One of these days, your uncle will have to bring you down to the lake. I'll take you for a spin in my boat."

"We'd love it!" Meg declared.

"That's a wonderful team," Uncle Hal remarked warmly, after he had closed the door. "I don't see how this community could get along without Doc Willoughby."

He went to the fireplace and stirred the coals with a poker. Meg and Kerry were dying to discuss the Hawthorne mystery, but before they could say a word, Uncle Hal went on talking about his friend.

"He first came to Merrybones about ten years ago, right out of training." Hal settled into one of the chairs, and the girls knelt down near his feet. "People wondered why a gifted doctor would settle in a poor community like this."

"Maybe they didn't have a doctor," said Kerry.

Meg's uncle smiled. "They didn't, Kerry. The old

doc who had treated them for years had died. I suppose Willoughby stayed simply because they did need him. Now they almost worship him. Dr. Willoughby and Della save more lives in a year than most medical men do in a lifetime.''

"Is she a real nurse?" asked Meg. It was hard to think of a nurse without a crisp white uniform.

"I think the doctor trained her himself, Meg. And she thinks the sun rises and sets on him—for a very good reason. When he first came to town, he saved the life of Della's only brother.

"It's a remarkable story," Uncle Hal continued. "The young man had fallen from a dangerous cliff. It was the dead of winter, and he was badly injured. Dr. Willoughby went down on ropes, treated him, and stayed with him until it was safe to bring him up. Doc almost died of the cold himself.''

"Uncle Hal—" There was a slight frown on Meg's young forehead. "If Dr. Willoughby is so kind and wonderful, why didn't Emily go to him for advice when she got those awful letters?''

Her uncle ran his fingers through his thick dark hair. "I don't know, Meg," he said. "She seems to have a feeling of doubt about all the people of this town. It's almost a superstition. She wouldn't even let me tell Officer Sykes.''

"Did you see him today?" both girls asked at once. "Did you learn anything new?" added Meg.

"Nothing too helpful, I'm afraid. But it may be a clue, and you'll be interested. I did talk to Sykes. He remembers the Hawthorne family.

"Emily's father worked in the Stoner lumber mill. When his wife died and the mill closed, he decided to take Emily and move away from Merrybones. The sad thing is that he died before they could leave."

"What did he die of?" Meg was instantly alert. Could there be some connection between the past and those threatening letters?

"Well, there was some mystery about it at first. But apparently he died of a heart attack. Someone found him unconscious in the woods one night and called the sheriff. The sheriff located him, still unconscious, just where the caller said he would be. But he died before they could get medical help. And no one ever found out who made that call."

"Were they sure it was a heart attack?"

"I went right to Dr. Willoughby," Uncle Hal replied. "Of course, he wasn't in Merrybones back then, but he still has the records of the old doctor. He wasn't particularly happy about divulging old family medical records at first, but finally he did. There's no doubt—Emily's father had a bad heart for years.

"There's another strange thing, though, Meg," he continued. "Hawthorne had just sold his home and was known to have had a large sum of cash in his pocket. But the money was gone and has never been found."

"Poor Emily," Kerry said softly. "What happened to her, Mr. Ashley?"

"Well, she must have been with her father that night. She was found wandering in the woods the next day. There had been a terrible storm; she was in a daze and too frightened to answer questions. However, she did say something about seeing a 'dark monster' in the woods. She doesn't even remember that night now."

Meg had a faraway look in her eyes. *A tiny child might call a witch a dark monster,* she thought with a shiver.

"Emily's aunt came from the West and took her away," Uncle Hal continued in a low voice. "She didn't come back for almost twenty years— But what about you two?" He had straightened up suddenly and changed the subject. "What happened to you today? Did you find any blueberries?"

"Did we?" Kerry couldn't stay quiet any longer. She jumped to her feet, her blue eyes sparkling. "We found a billion of them, and—"

"And that isn't all, Uncle Hal," Meg interrupted her friend. "I think *maybe* we saw Melissa today."

"Melissa? You mean Emily's lost cat? Meg—" he stood up, drawing her to her feet with him—"that's great news! I think Emily would quit brooding if she could get that old cat back."

"Well, I'm not sure," Meg said breathlessly. "But after we picked the berries, we went to Wigwam Cave and. . . ."

Taking turns, she and Kerry told him everything —how they had found the black-magic signs and the candles in the cave and how the little girl had appeared all of a sudden and then run away.

"We chased her and chased her," said Kerry. "But she hid somewhere around the old lumber mill, and we had to go back and get our berries and lunch."

"Do you know who the child was, Meg?" asked Uncle Hal.

Meg nodded. "Betsy thought her name was Lisa McKay. She's staying with her aunt at a house on the way to the cave. Betsy said it's called the Hawthorne house."

"I know the house, and I know Miss Bell," he said. "I heard in town that Cora Bell's sister was visiting her. That must be the sister's little girl. Are you sure, Meg, that the cat was black?"

"I'm positive, Uncle Hal. It was big and coal black, just like Emily said."

"Well, what are we waiting for?" Uncle Hal looked down at his watch, as excited now as his young listeners. "What do you say we check this out right now? I'll run down and see if I can borrow Clyde Stoner's jeep," he said. "Then we'll pick up Emily and dash out to that house. If we don't find the cat there, we'll look around the old mill. I only hope it really is Melissa."

Meg and Kerry beat him to the door. This was exactly what they had wanted.

Emily's face lit up like a star at the prospect of seeing her beloved pet again, although she didn't dare to hope too much.

"It could be Melissa, of course," she said, "but when I met Miss Bell in the drugstore last week, I asked her if she had seen my cat. She said, 'Certainly not!' In fact, she informed me that she's allergic to fur."

Hal was driving down a lane toward a small cottage with a shingled roof and wide porch. "Didn't this place once belong to your family, Emily?" he asked.

"Yes." The soft, pale hair blew back from her face

as she turned to him. "But I haven't been inside it since I left Merrybones as a little girl. Miss Bell and I work together at school, and I had hoped that she would invite me to visit her, but she hasn't. I—I'm afraid—" Emily hesitated—"I'm afraid she doesn't like me very much."

"She's probably jealous because you're so young and pretty," said the outspoken Kerry. The same thought had flashed through Meg's mind.

Hal stopped the jeep under a huge tree. He didn't say, "Stay here," when he opened the door for Emily, so Meg and Kerry tumbled out, too.

They followed Hal and the young teacher up the steps of the old Hawthorne house, where Emily had lived and played as a child.

6

A CAT NAMED MELISSA

Cora Bell was a tall, thin woman, wearing rimless glasses. She didn't seem too pleased at the sight of her unexpected visitors. She invited them in, but her manner was formal.

"I'm surprised to see you're still in town, Miss Hawthorne," she said to Emily. "I thought surely you would be rushing off to spend your vacation back in California."

Emily smiled. "Merrybones is my home now, Miss Bell. I wanted to be here for the blueberry social."

"We've really come in search of a lost cat, Miss Bell." Hal came right to the point. "Meg and Kerry, here, thought they saw a little girl in the woods today with a black cat. Does your sister's child own one?"

"A black cat?" The woman's lips tightened. "Certainly not," she said. "The girls must be mistaken. Lisa has no pets, and I assure you that she has been indoors with my sister most of the day.''

Just then, Lisa herself came tripping down the stairs. She was wearing black slippers now, and a prim little pink gingham dress. She smiled impishly when she saw Meg and Kerry.

"Hello," she said. "We ran away from you. You couldn't find us."

Meg and Kerry met her at the bottom of the steps. "You were hiding," said Meg seriously.

"And you had a black cat," said Kerry. "Where is it now?"

Lisa laughed. "That wasn't a cat," she teased. "It was a beautiful black princess. I put her in the castle."

"This is nonsense." Miss Bell came forward suddenly. "The child has a wild imagination. She's forever playacting. Lisa," she said sternly, "go upstairs and tell your mother tea will soon be ready."

The small girl hesitated. Then Hal spoke up. "May I speak to her, Miss Bell?"

She could hardly refuse, and Hal came and bent down beside Lisa. He was smiling.

"It wasn't really a princess, was it, Lisa?" he said. "It was a cat. Her name is Melissa, and she belongs to Miss Hawthorne." He pointed to the young woman. "She feels very sad because Melissa is lost. Can you show us where she is hiding?"

59

Lisa glanced briefly at Emily, regarded Hal soberly for a moment, then smiled. "All right. Come on!" Lisa whirled suddenly, like a pink butterfly, and went skipping to the door. The others followed her outside.

Only Miss Bell remained standing on the porch, while the rest went in search of Melissa. Miss Bell looked distinctly annoyed.

Behind the house was a large tract of woodland, through which Lisa led Emily, Hal, Meg, and Kerry. At the back edge of the woods were a number of old wooden outbuildings.

Lisa ran straight to one of them. She unlatched the rickety door, and Meg's uncle pulled it open. Out bounded the black cat.

"Oh, Melissa!" Emily was kneeling on the ground, waiting. The cat whimpered a little, trotted over to her, then leaped into her arms, purring noisily. Melissa was obviously happy to be free but none the worse for her imprisonment.

Meg and Kerry were as pleased by the rescue as Emily, but now Meg had some questions to ask. She took Lisa's hand as they trooped back to the house. "Where did you find Melissa?" she asked.

"In a tree," the child said. "She got away, and somebody tried to catch her. They talked in a high, mean voice."

"Did you see who it was?" Meg held her breath, awaiting the answer.

Lisa shook her head. "They went away fast in a car. I got some meat from Aunt Cora's house to feed the cat. I kept her out here because Aunt Cora doesn't like furry things."

Kerry was walking on the other side of her. "Did you light the candle in the cave, Lisa?" she asked warily.

"No," Lisa answered. "I'm not supposed to go there." Then her eyes grew big. "It was the *witches*," she whispered. With that, she broke away and ran toward the house.

Why did that word *witches* keep popping up? Meg looked blankly at Kerry. They were both more confused than ever.

Lisa's aunt looked at Melissa with distaste when Emily, with the cat in her arms, returned to the porch. Miss Bell scolded the child for having played alone in the woods, but she was plainly embarrassed at the turn things had taken. She suddenly surprised everyone by inviting Emily to go through the house.

"I know this used to be your home, Miss Hawthorne," she said stiffly. "Come in. But please leave that—that animal behind."

Emily, eager to accept the invitation, handed the big cat to Meg and followed Miss Bell through the door. When she returned minutes later, there was a curious stillness about her.

She's trying to remember what it was like long ago, thought Meg.

"I'd hate to have *that* woman for a teacher," said Kerry when they were once more in the jeep. "She must be the one who sent Emily those poison-pen letters."

"Wouldn't *that* be a development!" said Uncle Hal, laughing loudly. "Incidentally, did you see her face when Emily came back carrying the cat?" He chuckled, remembering Miss Bell's expression of distaste.

Emily smiled as she stroked Melissa, who was curled peacefully in her lap. "I'm sure Miss Bell would like for me to leave Merrybones," she said, "but she'd never stoop to writing unsigned threatening letters. And it *was* good of her to show me the house."

Meg wasn't so sure. She half suspected that the older teacher was covering up. She hadn't acted really surprised when they found the cat, Meg thought.

Kerry voiced their suspicion. "I bet she took Melissa herself. I bet she was going to drive into the woods with her and lose her, but the cat got away."

With the return of Melissa, the feeling of evil that hung over the Maine village seemed to vanish—at least for a time. For the next few days, Meg and Kerry were much too busy to worry about witches or black-magic signs.

Uncle Hal rented horses for them from Officer Sykes. Sykes was a wiry little man, who always spoke his mind. With some reluctance, he let the girls pick out the most spirited mounts. Kerry was in her glory as they rode up and down the streets of the town and around the lake.

When Betsy and Clyde Stoner weren't busy with chores at the big house, they sometimes went along. At those times, the girls were allowed to venture into the woods. One day they ate their picnic lunch beside a sparkling waterfall, while the horses grazed nearby.

But best of all, for Meg at least, were the jaunts on the lake. In spite of his heavy practice, Dr. Willoughby found time for his hobby. He had a power launch, and sometimes he invited Hal and the girls to go boating with him. Meg loved to spin across the water and feel the cold spray on her cheeks.

One afternoon Emily joined them. She had received no more of the threatening letters, and Meg and Kerry were delighted to see the color back in her face. She wore a very becoming blue scarf over her light hair.

Dr. Willoughby smiled at the sight of the young teacher. "If I may say so, Miss Hawthorne," he said gallantly, "you look radiant." He helped her into the boat. "You must be feeling better."

"Oh, yes!" said Emily, returning his smile.

"I'm afraid we owe it all to a cat named Melissa, Doctor," said Meg's uncle. He brought a chest of cold drinks aboard and stowed them under a seat. "Finding her pet was the tonic Emily needed."

The young woman laughed. "That isn't all of it,"

she insisted. She found a seat between Meg and Kerry and pushed the blue scarf down around her shoulders. "You remember, Dr. Willoughby, that I asked a lot of questions about my family when I first came back to Merrybones last year? Well, Cora Bell took me through my old home the other day. Now I —I seem to be getting my memory back! I can even see my father's face. . . ."

Dr. Willoughby was just about to start the motor. Meg happened to be looking at his back as Emily spoke.

At Emily's words, the man seemed to go rigid. His hand hung for a long second in midair. Then it came down, and he pulled the starter cord. The launch began to vibrate.

"It isn't good to think about the past, Miss Hawthorne," he called over his shoulder. "A pretty woman like you should be looking to the future."

With that, the boat leaped forward in the water. Meg gripped the rail. It was a most trivial incident, yet Meg suddenly had that *feeling*—that warning tingle at the back of her neck. Something in Emily Hawthorne's words had alarmed Dr. Willoughby.

Meg would have thought nothing more of the incident, had it not been for something that happened later that day.

The boat was swinging around the far end of the lake, and Uncle Hal pointed out an enormous mansion that was going to ruin. "You should have seen it fifteen years ago," the doctor shouted. "It was really a showplace then."

Fifteen years ago. Only Meg's sharp ears caught it. Of course, it could mean nothing at all—Dr. Willoughby might have seen a picture of the house. Still, Meg felt that he had seen it with his own eyes, although Uncle Hal had definitely told her and Kerry that the doctor first came to Merrybones *ten* years ago.

Could he have been here before that? Did he know something about Emily's childhood that he dared not reveal?

The idea was disturbing, but the day was particularly lovely, and Meg refused to think further about disturbing things.

7

THE LOCKED DOOR

Meg's feeling about Dr. Willoughby was really so vague that she didn't even mention it to Kerry. She realized by the next day that she could have just imagined that the doctor was disturbed when he learned that Emily was recovering her memory. Anyway, Kerry had her own theory—and a sound one, too—about Emily's problem.

"Emily thinks Miss Bell wouldn't *stoop* to writing those letters," Kerry said, "but I'm *sure* she's the guilty one. Betsy told me that, at the town meeting, the people of the town voted to make Emily principal of the school, because she has such a fine education. Miss Bell was hopping mad about it. She thought *she* should be principal."

Meg was startled by this new information. "It could be a motive," she admitted.

The girls were in their attic room at the big house.

Meg had been sitting at the desk, trying to write a letter to her father. Kerry paced restlessly around the room, talking about the unsolved mystery.

"Don't forget that Lisa found Emily's cat near the Bell house," Kerry insisted. "Her aunt could have lied about being allergic."

Meg nodded. "I've thought about that," she said.

"I just don't trust that woman. There's something creepy going on near there, and even little Lisa knows it. Remember what she said about the witches—"

"Oh, Kerry!" With a sigh, Meg put down her pen. "Lisa lives in a dream world. She runs off by herself and plays make-believe. Don't you remember how we used to pretend—"

"Shhhh!" Kerry broke in. "Somebody's coming."

The door opened, and Betsy popped into the room. She had been baby-sitting with the little Millard girl, who had been sick.

"How is Kim, Betsy?" asked Meg.

"Sassy!" Betsy answered, with an impish grin. "Ma says she just ate too many cookies, but Mrs. Millard is worried. Doc Willoughby and his nurse are going to stop in on their way somewhere and look at her. I came up to get some toys for her to play with," Betsy added. She opened the chest at the foot of the bed and took out the rag doll and a little music box.

69

She was about to leave, then suddenly turned back. "Something funny happened this morning," she said. "You know that fat little lady on the second floor? Her name is Mrs. Heebles. I was taking some towels to her room, and I thought she was down at breakfast, so I opened her door.

"You'll never guess. She was trying on the craziest outfit—a long, black, ugly dress. When she saw me, she looked real mad. She grabbed the towels and slammed the door in my face."

Meg stood up. "A long black dress," she repeated slowly. "I wonder—"

"She's probably going to a party," Kerry said impatiently. "Come on, Meg," she begged. "I'm bored. Let's go with Betsy and help entertain Kim. You can sing songs and dance, and I can make funny faces."

She promptly made a very funny one. Meg had to give in and laugh. She decided to finish her letter later, and so the three scrambled together down the stairs.

Passing the door of the living room, they heard voices and paused to peer in. A group of women were sitting there, chatting and giggling like a bunch of girls. Mrs. Heebles was among them, and—to Meg's surprise—so was Mrs. Stoner. Betsy's mother was almost never seen without her apron and broom—

and she was seldom seen smiling or laughing.

"Those are Ma's old friends," whispered Betsy. "They went to school together up in Boston, years and years ago. Sometimes they get together for reunions. Come on," she said.

Just then the old-fashioned doorbell chimed. "I'll get it," cried Meg, who was closest. "You and Kerry go along."

She ran down the hall to open the door—and there was another surprise! Miss Cora Bell stood on the porch, holding a large dress box in her arms. When she saw Meg, she acted as though she wanted to hide it.

The tall woman glared coldly at Meg for a moment, then swept past her. "I came to call on Betsy's mother," she snapped and marched on down the hall in the direction of the laughing voices.

Meg couldn't resist tiptoeing back for another look. Cora Bell was handing the box to Mrs. Stoner and smiling now, in a very friendly way. Then someone noticed Meg in the doorway, and a dead silence fell over the room.

Flushing with embarrassment, Meg ran off to join Kerry and Betsy. They played with the little sick girl for a full hour, until she fell asleep. Then Kerry and Betsy went down to wade in the lake, and Meg went back upstairs to finish her letter to her father.

She had much to tell him. Mr. Duncan was presently at his government office in Washington, and he enjoyed getting Meg's long, interesting letters.

The events in Merrybones were certainly becoming more interesting—and more mysterious—all the time, and Meg was beginning to think that part of the mystery was centered in this very house.

She was still pondering that disturbing theory when she drifted off to sleep that night.

It must have been about midnight when she was awakened by an unusual noise. She opened her eyes in the darkness, listening. The sound was coming from behind the door to the other part of the attic!

That door had always been locked, and Meg had often wondered what lay beyond it. One day, when she ran into the room to get her colored glasses, she had thought, for an instant, that she heard someone in there.

Startled now, she jumped out of bed. The door was slightly ajar, and she could see a light. As she started cautiously toward it, the door swung wide open. Meg found herself standing face-to-face with Betsy's mother!

Mrs. Stoner was plainly flustered at seeing Meg. "Oh, I—I'm sorry, Meg," she said. "I was so sure you two girls were sound asleep. This—this is the only way to get into the storeroom, and I had to put something away. I thought I'd slip in without waking you. . . ."

All the while, she was working her way toward the exit. Now she vanished through the door, and Meg heard her steps on the stairway.

In her confusion, Mrs. Stoner had forgotten to re-lock the door to the storeroom.

8
A BOOK OF BLACK MAGIC

By now Kerry was awake. She had been curious, too, about what was beyond that locked door. When Meg told her what had happened, she couldn't be stopped.

Kerry got a tiny flashlight out of her suitcase, and she and Meg crept cautiously into the dark room. It was a perfect New England storeroom, neat as a pin.

For some reason, Meg felt let down. Then Kerry cast her light on a row of shelves. There it was—the dress box Miss Bell had brought to the house—and from one corner of it hung a flap of black cloth.

"Let's hurry, before she comes back," whispered Kerry. Handing the flashlight to Meg, she pushed a stool over to the shelves. She climbed up and brought the big box down.

Trembling, they opened it on the floor. By now Meg wasn't too much surprised at what it held: a witch's costume, with a folded pointed hat and a black mask.

"Look, Kerry!" Meg cried softly as she lifted the hat. "Here's a book!"

She picked it up and held it close to the light. It was a small book, very old and shabby. It was bound in leather, and the pages were stiff and spotted with age.

Meg looked at the first page. *"Ye Booke of fpellf,"* she read, sounding the words as they were printed.

"fpellf?" echoed Kerry in disgust. "What does *that* mean?"

Meg was almost choking with excitement. "It's written in Old English," she whispered. "Uncle Hal has shown me books like this at the museum. The *s*'s are written like *f*'s, and some of the words we use have the *e* at the end. Those *e*'s are pronounced like *y*. And that little word *ye* is really the same as our word *the,"* she added, pointing to the page. "The Booky of Spells." She read it again, carefully, the way it was meant to sound.

"Well, what kind of a silly booky is *that?"* Kerry whispered back, giggling helplessly.

Meg's eyes met her friend's in the dim light. "Don't laugh, Kerry," she said in an awed voice. "I think we've found a book of black magic!"

She turned the pages slowly, trying her best to make out the ancient printing. She felt a chill crawl along her neck.

Ye convene shalle be some thirteen witches . . . . They shalle meet in ye fulle of ye moone for to make a sabbate and for to performe ye magic spells.

Again Meg looked up. "It says that thirteen witches make a *coven,* Kerry. And when they have a meeting to make their magic, that is called a *Sabbat.* This little book tells how they go about making their magic."

The book was filled with recipes for witches' brews, with horrible ingredients in them. It had spells with numbers and letters, and spells with herbs. Meg translated as she whispered the awful words:

"Rosemary, thyme, and bitter rue.
A witch's evil curse on you."

When she came near the end of the book, a piece of paper fell out onto the floor. Meg unfolded it. Her eyes grew wide.

76

On the paper was a list of names, written in odd brownish ink. They were strange, exotic names—Circe, Cassandra, Endorella, Tituba, Felina, Grimalkina. . . . There were thirteen in all.

Meg handed the paper to Kerry. "What do you think of that?"

Kerry swallowed. "They sound like witches' names," she said in a shivery voice. "You said you saw Miss Bell bring this box to Betsy's mother. Do you suppose *they*. . . ."

"I don't know." Meg put the paper carefully back where it belonged, at the end of the book. "I sure wish we could show this to Uncle Hal."

"Let's take it!"

"I wouldn't dare. Don't forget the awful things that have been happening to Emily Hawthorne. I wouldn't want them mad at *us*."

Meg was just putting the book and hat back into the box when there was a sound from the second floor. A door creaked as it opened.

"Quick!" cried Meg. "Put the box back!"

They acted just in time. Kerry jumped up and shoved the box into place. Then she pushed the stool against the wall.

They were back in bed, eyes innocently closed, when the door of their room was opened once more.

Meg heard stealthy footsteps cross the floor, then a tiny metallic *click*.

Mrs. Stoner had remembered the unlocked door.

Kerry had been fascinated by the strange writing in the ancient *Book of Spells*. Next morning at breakfast, she whispered to Meg. "Pleafe paff ye falt," sounding her *s*'s like *f*'s.

Meg laughed and took up the salt to pass to her friend. "Here it if," she whispered back. "Put it on your eggf, and mind your mannerf. And be careful," she added warningly. "Here comes Mrs. Stoner herself!"

Young Mrs. Millard, who was nearby with her little girl, looked at them as if they were daffy. Kerry, giggling, choked on a bit of toast, and Meg had to pound her on the back.

Uncle Hal didn't come to the big house for breakfast that day. As soon as they had eaten, Meg and Kerry dashed up the hill to the cabin to tell him what had happened during the night.

Hal listened in silence to their weird story and didn't laugh at all. In fact, he took it very seriously.

"Look, Meg," he said. "In spite of Emily's desire for secrecy, I think it's about time we called Officer Sykes in on this case. This is my first chance to tell

you: Emily's cat disappeared again last night.''

Meg and Kerry looked at him in dismay. "Was she stolen again?'' asked Kerry.

"We can't be sure of that, but Emily is terribly upset. She ran around for hours searching for the cat. This dreadful business has her so nervous that she's almost sick. I asked Doc Willoughby's nurse to go and sit with her last night.

"And that isn't all," he added worriedly. He walked over to the fireplace. "Did either of you pick up those gray stones I found at Wigwam Cave?''

Meg and Kerry shook their heads.

"Well, somebody did. One was on the mantel, and I'm sure I put the other one right there on the coffee table. Of course, anybody could have walked in—I seldom lock the door. The stones are absolutely worthless; it's mighty odd that anyone would want them badly enough to steal them.''

Meg and Kerry looked at each other, completely bewildered. Mysterious things seemed to be happening one right after another, and none of them made any sense at all.

"I think you're right, Uncle Hal," Meg said anxiously. "Officer Sykes knows more about this town than we do. Maybe he can figure all this out.''

9

A SLIGHT ACCIDENT

"Witches in Merrybones?"

Officer Sykes was sitting in his office at the riding stables, whittling on a piece of wood. He tipped his head back and chuckled good-naturedly when Meg told him what she and Kerry had found in Mrs. Stoner's attic.

"That's about the wildest thing I ever heard," he said. "Why, I've known Mrs. Stoner all my life. She's a no-nonsense woman if I ever met one." He turned to Hal. "Mr. Ashley, do you honestly expect me to start accusing the fine ladies of this town of being witches?"

"I think you should look into the matter, Mr. Sykes," Meg's uncle said seriously. "A great many people *are* trying to delve into the occult these days. Please read these poison-pen letters once more." He offered them to Sykes for the second time. "If we don't act, I'm afraid Miss Hawthorne will be frightened into leaving Merrybones. You can't afford to lose such a fine teacher."

Sykes pushed the letters aside. "No need for me to read 'em again," he said. "They're just crank letters. I hear tell Miss Hawthorne is a tough grader. Some young feller who didn't pass his English is trying to get her goat."

"Meg, come here!" Kerry had slipped away and was petting one of the horses tied nearby. When Meg came, looking troubled, Kerry said, "Let's go see Emily this morning, Meg. Maybe we can take her riding with us and make her feel better."

Meg thought it was a fine idea. So did Uncle Hal, who, obviously annoyed with Officer Sykes, had joined them.

"While you two are cheering Emily up," he said, when they had moved far enough away that Sykes couldn't hear, "I'm going to visit one or two of her students. She did mention a lad who liked to play pranks. If that fails, I'll go to Mrs. Stoner myself."

Emily was glad to see the girls, although it was apparent that she had been crying and that she was extremely nervous. At first she refused their invitation to go riding.

"Please come," Meg urged. "It'll be such fun—and we might even find Melissa."

At mention of Melissa, Emily agreed at once, and she returned to the stables with the girls. Mr. Sykes's helper had already saddled three horses—at Hal's request.

They rode for two hours, around the lake and up near the old lumber mill. They didn't find the lost Melissa, but they did work up ravenous appetites.

"I'll fix us all something to eat," said Emily when they had returned to her cottage. "I didn't feel like eating breakfast this morning." She looked much brighter now but plainly didn't want the girls to leave her alone. She went into the kitchen.

Meg phoned Mrs. Stoner, to tell her that she and Kerry wouldn't be at the big house for lunch. As she turned from the telephone, she heard a cabinet door open.

An instant later she heard a scream.

Meg and Kerry ran into the kitchen. A cabinet door was open, and Emily was lying on the floor in front of the sink. There was an angry red spot on her forehead, and she appeared to be unconscious.

Something had frightened her, and, in jumping aside, she must have slipped on the highly polished floor and hit her head on a counter.

"Oh, oh—" Kerry knelt down on the floor beside the injured girl, but Meg was staring into the cabinet.

On the shelf sat Betsy Stoner's old rag doll, an impish grin on its face. At the doll's feet lay one of the black-magic stones.

There was no time now to think of what all this meant. "You stay with her, Kerry," Meg said quickly. "I'll run and get Dr. Willoughby."

Fortunately, the doctor's office was just a few doors away. Meg burst into the waiting room without knocking.

Della Armstrong was there alone. She was sitting in an upholstered chair, holding a small blue book in her hands. Taken completely by surprise, she looked startled and confused. She thrust the book out of sight between the seat cushion and arm and stood up, her hands behind her.

Now in a white uniform, she seemed much more like a real nurse. She appeared worried, and Meg soon discovered why.

"Oh, dear," she protested, when Meg begged to see the doctor, "he's finally gone to sleep. He spent all night with a patient over in Surrey, and I wasn't there to help. . . . He's so overworked that he's even thinking of leaving Merrybones—"

"But he has to come," Meg interrupted, her tone

urgent. "Emily might be seriously hurt!"

"Yes, of course. I'm sorry." The gray-haired woman bit her lip. Then she whisked away to summon the doctor.

Meg sat down in the chair, where her nervous fingers soon came upon the book the nurse had been holding. Absently she glanced at it. She was surprised to discover that it was a small diary. She put it back at once, of course. But she wondered what dramatic thing Miss Armstrong had been recording when she was interrupted.

The doctor arrived a moment later, putting on his jacket. He did look haggard, and Meg felt sorry for him. He hurriedly picked up his bag, and they set out at once.

By the time they reached Emily's small cottage, the girl had come to. She was lying on the couch, her eyes closed. Kerry was holding a cold cloth to Emily's forehead.

The doctor bent over her and took her hand. "Emily," he said gently.

Her eyes flew open. They were full of fear, and she began to tremble, but when she saw that it was the doctor, she calmed down.

"I—I'm sorry, Dr. Willoughby," she whispered. "I've been having bad dreams about when I was a little girl. I keep seeing my father—someone bending over him—"

"Don't talk now," the doctor said firmly. He examined her eyes with his light.

There was a tiny drop of blood on the injury now; he cleansed it thoroughly, then covered it with sterile gauze and tape. He gave her some tablets for her nerves.

"The injury isn't serious." Meg was listening as the doctor talked with her uncle on the porch of Emily's cottage. Hal had dropped in to see Emily and had learned of the accident.

"I'm glad of that," Hal said. "She's had a lot to worry her lately." He didn't explain.

"Miss Hawthorne is a sensitive young woman," said Dr. Willoughby. "It isn't easy to make friends in this town, and I know she's been lonely. In fact, I strongly advised her to go back to the West Coast, where life was more pleasant for her."

The doctor's face was turned from her, but once again Meg had that warning tingle at the back of her neck. He sounded almost as though he *wanted* Emily out of Merrybones. That didn't make sense—did it?

He stepped down from the porch. "I'm going to close the office and try to get some sleep, folks. I'll

send Della over to check on Emily, so you girls can leave,'' he said to Meg.

While they were waiting for the nurse, Meg and Kerry slipped into the kitchen. They put the rock and the rag doll into a paper sack and took them away when they left. They didn't want poor Emily to come upon them and be frightened all over again.

"How did she happen to fall?'' Hal asked as they walked back to his cabin.

Meg showed him the contents of the sack. "Somebody put these in her kitchen cupboard, where she'd be sure to see them.''

"She got frightened and slipped,'' said Kerry.

Uncle Hal paused to study the rag doll with the button eyes and blond hair. His lips tightened.

"This is too much," he spat out angrily. "Now they walk right into her house to threaten her! This doll and the stone were probably put in the cupboard while you three were riding."

"It could have been before, Mr. Ashley," said Kerry. "Emily told us she had a lot of visitors yesterday: some of her old pupils, and the egg man—and even old Miss Bell, who came to bring her some school records."

"Well, that's Betsy's doll," declared Meg. "And whoever took it and put it in Emily's house must be the same one who wrote the letters. This is a warning that something bad will happen if she doesn't go away."

"That's the vicious thing about witchcraft, Meg," said Uncle Hal. "It isn't the spells that harm people —it's the fear. In primitive tribes, the witch doctors can often make accidents happen just by the power of suggestion. If a man *thinks* something bad will happen, and if he worries about it long enough, his own fear makes the witch's curse come true."

"Well, Emily is scared enough, all right," said Kerry solemnly. "When she came to, she told me she just couldn't stand it anymore. She's going away—

just as soon as she finds Melissa again.''

"We're not going to let her do that," said Hal.

They had reached the cabin door. For once the door was locked. Hal got out his key and let Meg and Kerry in. Then he stood on the stoop for a long moment, thinking.

"We've been getting exactly nowhere, Meg," he said finally. "If Officer Sykes refuses to act, we'll have to take matters into our own hands. Now I'm going down to the Stoner house and ask a few questions.''

Meg stared at him. "Are you going to tell Mrs. Stoner about the box Kerry and I found in the attic, Uncle Hal?''

"No. I don't want to get you two in bad with her. You really had no business snooping in that storeroom, Meg, though it might be a lucky thing that you did. I intend to show her the poison-pen letters, and I'll ask her point-blank if she knows who mailed them to Emily—and why.''

10

THE FULL OF
THE MOON

Meg and Kerry waited anxiously in the cabin while
Uncle Hal visited the Stoner house. He was gone for
almost an hour. When he returned, he looked puzzled and a little angry.

"What did Mrs. Stoner say?" asked Meg.

"Not very much." His tone was sharp. "She said
she knew absolutely nothing about those letters.
When I mentioned witchcraft, she got on her high
horse. She said there hadn't been a witch in Maine
since back in the seventeen hundreds, when some
poor old preacher was hanged for witchcraft. But
there was something very suspicious about the way
she acted."

"Do you think she was telling the truth?" asked
Kerry.

"It's hard to believe that a strict New England
woman like Mrs. Stoner could be mixed up in an

ugly affair like this. Still, you can't always tell about people. I'm almost sure she was lying, Kerry.''

"Well, Kerry and I know that she *did* put the witch costume in the attic," said Meg.

"If it weren't for Emily," Uncle Hal went on, "we'd fly out of this place right now. But we can't desert a friend. Now, you kids watch your step," he warned. "Try not to stir up any trouble. After supper, I'll have another talk with Sykes. I'm sure that when he learns about Emily's accident, he'll decide that this matter is worth investigating.''

Meg and Kerry didn't go back to the big house right away. They spent the rest of the afternoon with Meg's uncle, feeding the squirrels and playing Scrabble. By the time they went down the hill, the moon was coming up over the lake.

The moon was full, and suddenly Meg had a dreadful feeling that something was going to happen this very night. Would the "coven" of witches meet in the full of that moon? Would they hold their mysterious "Sabbat" to work their fearful spells?

Mrs. Stoner, her eyes glittering with a curious light, didn't even speak to the girls during dinner. Tension hung over the table . . . over the entire gaunt, gray house.

Afterward, several unusual things happened. First,

Mrs. Stoner had a mysterious call and told Betsy that she was going to have to spend the night with a sick neighbor. Then Cora Bell came in with her little niece, Lisa. She asked if the child could stay the night, because she and her sister had to take an urgent trip.

There was an extra bed in the tiny room where the Millard girl slept; Mrs. Millard kindly let Lisa stay there.

Meg herself was so restless that she couldn't sleep at all when she went to bed. She got up finally and wandered around the room. When she looked at the clock, it was half past eleven. For some time she had thought she heard furtive noises in the house.

Now she heard a door open and close in the lower hall—then the sound of motors outside. She ran to look out the window. Two cars were coming from the direction of the hotel on the hill. They were creeping along with their lights out!

One of the cars stopped a short distance from the Stoner house. Several shadowy figures ran to it and got inside. Two of them seemed to be carrying suitcases. Then the cars moved on down the street and out of sight, in the direction of the woods.

Meg wasted no time in waking up Kerry. They dressed in the dark, jumping into their clothes so fast that they scarcely had time to tie their sneakers.

"Let's go get Uncle Hal," Meg whispered.

They slipped out of the darkened house and ran up the hill to the cabin. To their dismay, they found Hal gone.

"Maybe he's still with Officer Sykes," said Meg.

"What'll we do now?" asked Kerry. "There's no time to go looking for him, and we don't dare to go into the woods alone when it's so dark. . . ."

Meg hesitated, then cried, "I've got an idea, Kerry! Come on back to the house."

They met Betsy Stoner, in her robe, poking around the downstairs hall. "What's going on?" she demanded to know. "Ma isn't home, and I heard a lot of noises. When I looked out of my room, I saw Mrs. Heebles. She was walking down the hall with a suitcase!"

Meg didn't quite know what to tell her. She didn't want to say that she thought Betsy's mother had lied about spending the night with a sick neighbor, but she had to make *some* explanation to get the girl's help.

As simply as she could, she told about the threatening letters Emily Hawthorne had received. "Someone in this town is trying to frighten her into going away, Betsy," she added.

94

"We think it's witches," said Kerry importantly. "Meg saw a bunch of people come down from the hotel in two cars. They drove up toward the Hawthorne house, where Miss Bell lives. She's one of them, too, I bet, and so is her sister."

"There aren't any witches," scoffed Betsy. But her voice was shaking, and her eyes looked big and scared in the dim hall light. "Besides, nobody would want to hurt Miss Hawthorne. Clyde and I think she's the best teacher ever."

"You just don't know all we do," declared Meg seriously. "If you really like Emily and want her to stay in Merrybones, Betsy, you'd better help us. Do you think your brother would take us out to Miss Bell's place in his jeep? We can spy on that meeting and find out just what's going on."

"I—I don't know," said Betsy doubtfully. "My brother gets awful mad when you wake him up. But we can try."

11
THIRTEEN WITCHES

"Witches?"

Clyde Stoner stuck an angry young face through the narrow opening of his door. "Are you kids nuts? Waking a guy up at this hour with a stupid story like that! No, I *won't* drive you to Miss Bell's house. Get back to bed!"

"Wait, Clyde." Meg grabbed the doorknob and stuck one foot in the door. "We haven't told you everything. Kerry and I found their book—a real book of black magic." She didn't dare to tell him *where* they had found it. "The witches are probably having a secret meeting right this very minute. And they might be planning more mischief for Emily. She's so scared now that she's about ready to go away—"

Clyde had been listening reluctantly. Now a look of doubt crossed his face. He pushed back his tousled hair. "I don't think Ma would like it, Betsy—"

"If you *don't* take us," Kerry broke in, "we'll go by ourselves."

"We can't ask Ma about it," said Betsy. "You know very well she's gone to sit with somebody sick. Please come, Clyde." Betsy herself was so convinced by now that she was almost in tears. "We *have* to help Miss Hawthorne. You can be the leader. We'll do exactly what you say."

"Oh, all right. Give me time to dress."

"I'll dress, too." Betsy ran to her room.

Meg and Kerry waited impatiently at the front door until the two came down.

It wasn't far to the cottage where Miss Bell lived. Before they got to the lane, Clyde switched off the headlights. He parked the jeep in the woods, where it wasn't likely to be spotted.

The four young people jumped to the ground and stole toward the house. The moon was bright, and they tried to keep well in the shadow of the trees.

Meg wasn't at all surprised to see lights in the place. Silhouetted figures could be seen moving about behind the window curtains.

Suddenly the front door swung open.

"Out of sight!" Meg ordered in a whisper. Just in time, all four dropped down behind the shrubbery.

Meg could see the door through the branches.

Through the door came an eerie figure—a tall form in a flowing black robe and pointed hat. A half mask disguised the face.

"That's wild!" muttered Clyde, crouching beside Meg. Meg couldn't answer. She was speechless with awe.

One by one, the witches were coming through the door and moving down the path that led into the forest. Each was dressed in a robe of black; each carried a lighted black candle. The flickering light played over the haggish faces.

One, two, three—Meg counted silently—*four, five, six. . . .* There were short ones, tall ones, thin ones, and fat ones—thirteen witches in all! It was a coven, complete. One witch carried a long, thin wand. The last in line held a shaggy broom over her shoulder. It was the strangest sight the four onlookers had ever seen.

"Do you suppose all thirteen are going to ride that one broomstick?" asked Clyde, when he had recovered a bit from the shock.

Kerry managed a strangled giggle, but she was more scared than amused, and so was Betsy.

Meg was silent. She still didn't quite believe what she had seen. Were they women she had passed on

98

the streets of Merrybones? Were they respectable housewives by day and blackhearted crones by night?

"Let's follow them," Meg suggested in a low voice. "But be careful—don't let them see you. I don't think they'd like to have their secrets known."

It wasn't hard to keep out of sight. The witches looked neither to the right nor to the left. They made their way slowly along the moonlit trail and over the bridge that crossed the stream.

Meg wasn't surprised at all when they headed straight for Wigwam Cave—the place of the legendary witch doctors who had made the bones of giants dance.

As they reached the entrance to the rocky cavern, each robed figure stopped to take off her shoes. Then, one by one, they disappeared from sight.

"What do we do now?" asked Betsy in a squeaky little voice.

Meg remembered something. "I know what I'm going to do," she said determinedly. "There's a hole at the top of the cave, where the rocks don't come together. I'm going to climb up there and peek in, if I can. I want to know what these weirdies are up to."

They picked their way silently around the rock pyramid, looking for a way up. In the rear, the stone slabs slanted down at an easy angle. The edges were jagged, and Meg felt sure she could find a foothold.

It wasn't too difficult. She had fine balance, from her years of ballet practice. Up she went, as sure-footed as a young Indian. She was grateful for her rubber-soled shoes. They were silent, and they gripped the uneven surface. She crawled atop her own shadow, for the full moon was at her back.

Meg held her breath as she reached the opening between the rocks. Cautiously she drew herself up the last few inches. Her dark braids brushed the stone as she peered down into the cave.

A chilling sight met her gaze. The thirteen black-clad figures stood in a circle, holding their candles high. As Meg watched, the one with the broom left the circle. She put her candle down on the flat rock and began to sweep the floor of the cave with extravagant flourishes of the broom.

As she swept, she chanted a mystical verse in a high, shrill voice. It made no sense at all to Meg, but it sounded like this:

> "Ammity, bammity, clammity, doh!
> Ekitty, feddity, greggity, hoh!"

The hag returned to the circle, and one of her sisters came forward. She was the one with the wand.

She put her candle down and, with the wand, drew an enormous figure on the floor of the cave—a pentacle, of course.

Now the remaining witches put down their candles, and the tallest witch of all stepped inside the pentacle. She held up her arms, and her black-clad sisters began to dance around her in a wild, unrestrained frenzy.

Meg was so fascinated by this behavior that she forgot all about her friends, who had remained below.

The dance went on for some time. Suddenly the tall witch lowered her arms, and the others froze in their tracks, as if stricken. Then began a mysterious ceremony.

The leader of the witches reached inside one of the enormous sleeves of her black robe. She drew out a small book. Meg caught her breath when she saw that it was the very same book of black magic she and Kerry had found in the attic.

The tall witch read from the book and put it beside the candles. Now she drew forth another object. To Meg, it looked like a lock of long blond hair, tied with black ribbon.

The witch waved it just above the candle flames. Then she flung a handful of powder into the flames.

All the while she was shouting, in a loud and terrible voice:

> "Rosemary, thyme, and bitter rue.
> A witch's evil curse on you."

An acrid smell rose from the flames, and Meg turned cold. Was that a lock of Emily's hair? she wondered. Was the dreadful curse meant for *Emily?*

Meg was so upset by now that she forgot to be careful. The moon had risen directly above the opening in the rocks. Her head was in the path of its rays, and it cast a foreign shadow on the floor of the cave below.

She jerked her head back. The shadow moved on the floor. Suddenly all the masked faces were turned up, toward the opening.

"Hecate, Hecate, goddess of the moon," the tall witch had been shouting. "Goddess of darkness—"

She stopped short and screamed a warning. Then all the witches were screeching together.

Meg had been discovered!

12

A JEEPFUL OF SHOES

Hecate was the moon goddess and the goddess of witchcraft in the old Greek legends—Meg knew that. And she was sure those women down there knew that *she* was no goddess!

As fast as she could, Meg clambered back down the rock stairway. Her heart was beating like a tom-tom. In her haste, she scraped her leg. She felt warm blood dripping down to her ankle.

Three white faces were upturned toward her as she made her descent. Clyde reached out and grabbed her and drew her safely to the ground.

"What happened, Meg?"

"They saw me!" she squealed. "Come on; let's get out of here!"

She started to run, then realized that her friends were not following. Turning, she saw that they were all hastily picking up something from the ground.

With their arms loaded, they caught up with her. All four went, running and stumbling, in the direction of the bridge and the jeep.

While Meg had been eavesdropping on the witches' "Sabbat," the others had not been idle. Kerry and Betsy and Clyde had gathered up all the shoes the foolish witches had left at the cave entrance, and now they were running off with them!

When they reached the jeep, they dumped thirteen pairs of shoes in the back. "We'll show 'em to Officer Sykes," said Clyde triumphantly. "He'll find out which witch fits which shoes. With this evidence, we'll catch 'em for sure!"

"They'll be furious when they find their shoes gone," Meg gasped, with a shiver. She got into the jeep, and, as they drove off, she described what she had seen in the rocky cavern.

"Some of them must have been there that day we found the candle burning in the cave, Kerry," she said. "Little Lisa must have been watching, too."

"Was Mrs. Heebles one of the witches?" asked Betsy. "I saw her leave the house—"

Meg nodded. "She's so short and fat that she couldn't even hide in a witch's costume. And Miss Bell was there, too, of course. She's the leader, I think. She stood inside the pentacle and shouted the curse, and she threw incense or something onto the candles."

"I knew it all the time," cried Kerry. *"She's* the one who wrote the poison-pen letters."

Meg's face was thoughtful in the darkness. It now seemed more than likely that Kerry's suspicions were right. Miss Bell did resent the younger teacher. Had she talked her gang of mischief-makers into putting a spell on Emily so she'd leave Merrybones?

"What do we do now, Meg?" asked Clyde as they came in sight of the Stoner house.

As it happened, Meg didn't have to decide that. When they drove up near the porch, they found Uncle Hal waiting for them. With him was Officer Sykes.

Uncle Hal seldom got angry with Meg—he knew she had a lot of good sense and could usually take care of herself—but right now he was pretty annoyed. He came around to the side of the jeep and opened the door for the girls.

"What are you kids doing, running around in the woods in the middle of the night?" he demanded. "I didn't have a chance to talk with Mr. Sykes right after supper. He'd been called away. When I did get to him and told him of Emily's fall, we came right over here to see Mrs. Stoner."

"And found her gone!" Sykes had come up behind Uncle Hal.

"Ma's out helping nurse a—a sick friend," said Betsy. Her little face looked stark and white in the moonlight. Was she beginning to suspect the truth about her own mother?

"Be that as it may," continued the officer, "we knocked on every door in your house, and nobody was home, except that young Millard couple and two little girls—and one old man who came up for the fishing."

"I'm terribly sorry, Uncle Hal," Meg said contritely. "But I saw them leaving the house and going into the woods. Kerry and I couldn't find you, so we got Clyde to take us—"

"Wait a minute, Meg." Uncle Hal may have been upset, but he was always fair and ready to listen. "Whom do you mean by *them?* Take a deep breath, honey, and tell us everything that happened—from the beginning."

Meg hardly knew how to begin. It all seemed like a wild nightmare now. But finally she got it out—just as it had happened.

"And we can prove it all, too, Mr. Ashley," said Clyde Stoner. "Just look in there." He reached into the jeep and pulled out a woman's shoe.

"We stole all their shoes—thirteen pairs!"

Even Uncle Hal had to smile at that.

107

Officer Sykes walked around the jeep to look in at the other side. "Well, I'll be danged," he said. "You kids sure had your wits about you. We've got the goods on 'em now."

"Go back into the house now, all of you," said Uncle Hal. He gave Meg a comforting little hug. "We'll take over from here."

Meg and Kerry followed Betsy and her brother meekly into the house. As Meg went up the stairway to their attic room, she felt suddenly tired. The scrape on her leg smarted, and she was alarmed at the hornet's nest she and Kerry had stirred up.

What would happen now? And what would poor Clyde and Betsy do when they found out that their own mother had been practicing witchcraft?

Meg locked the door of the room from the inside, but she and Kerry didn't go right back to bed. They leaned out of the window, anxiously watching the road below.

When the two big cars came creeping out of the woods back to the Stoner house, with their headlights off, Officer Sykes stepped down from the porch. He held up his hand, and both cars came to a stop.

Out of one stepped several dejected barefoot women. They were in ordinary clothes now. They stood there while Officer Sykes read them the riot act.

It was long and loud. Before he left, Mr. Sykes took down all of their names.

"I want all you ladies right here at the Stoner house at nine tomorrow morning," he shouted finally. "I'll inform Cora Bell and her sister. We're going to get to the bottom of this business, once and for all, and stop the mischief-making in this town.

"And don't any of you try to get away," he added, as some of the women limped toward the porch. "We've got the evidence against you. And if the shoes fit—you're going to wear 'em!"

The second car started up and drove slowly toward the hotel on the hill.

Kerry was shivering. Meg took her arm. "Come to bed, Kerry. Let's worry about it tomorrow," she said. "Those witches have a lot of explaining to do. They're going to need their *Booky of fpellf* to get out of *this* meff."

"Oh, Meg," protested Kerry, "how can you joke? Some of those witches will be sleeping in this very house!"

13

SWORN TO SECRECY

Once more the mysterious coven came together. Promptly at nine o'clock the following morning, thirteen women filed into the living room of the big house.

Some of them were women whom Meg knew. Some were strangers who had been staying at the hotel. Cora Bell was there, looking haughty and angry and embarrassed, all at the same time. With her was her sister. Guilt was written on all the faces.

Uncle Hal and Officer Sykes were there to receive them, along with Kerry—and Meg, who had witnessed the black revels in the cave.

The bedraggled-looking shoes were piled in the middle of the floor, and the "witches" gathered around them. Red with humiliation, each one picked out her own pair.

"Meg Duncan told me yesterday that people in Merrybones might be practicing witchcraft," Officer

Sykes said. "I told her the idea was pure nonsense. But there is no doubt in my mind now. Mrs. Stoner," he asked sternly, "how long has this been going on?"

"Oh, dear!" The woman looked so distressed that Meg felt almost sorry for her. "I'm afraid it's been going on for—for close to twenty years," she said. "But, believe me, Officer Sykes," she added desperately, "we meant no harm by it."

"That's true, Officer." Several of the women spoke at once.

"It was just an innocent game," fat little Mrs. Heebles said tearfully.

"An innocent game!" retorted the outraged lawman. "Do you call it innocent to send poison-pen letters through the mail and to drive a fine young woman nearly out of her wits with fear?"

"Poison-pen letters?" gasped one of the women in horror.

"Yes," said Sykes. He pulled the two letters from his pocket. Slowly and clearly, he read the threats aloud. Then he looked up with cold eyes. "Don't pretend you didn't try to put a hex on that poor young woman," he said.

Meg was puzzled. Except for Mrs. Stoner—who had learned about the letters from Hal and now stood rigidly silent—the women appeared truly stunned.

They were looking at each other in bewilderment. When Officer Sykes brought forth the rag doll, every one of the women shook her head.

"Why, that's Betsy's old rag doll," said Mrs. Stoner. "I haven't seen it in months. You say it was found at Miss Hawthorne's house? How ever did it get there?

"As for *that,*" she added when Sykes held up the black-magic stone, "we did make those. We each had one for good luck. But we never used them to *hex* anyone—"

"Miss Hawthorne is terrified by all this," Meg's uncle put in quietly. "If you ladies know anything, please speak out."

"But we don't know anything about that." Miss Bell lifted her thin face defiantly. "How could you gentlemen think we would stoop to such tricks? I don't particularly approve of Miss Hawthorne, as a teacher or as a principal, but I could never try to harm her—nor could my friends!"

"Her pupils love her," insisted Mrs. Stoner. "Maybe some of us women haven't been as neighborly as we might have been. Takes quite a spell for Maine folks to thaw out with newcomers. But we certainly did not put a curse on her."

"Then who in thunder did?" shouted Mr. Sykes,

112

losing his temper. "And if you *didn't,* what were you all doing up at Wigwam Cave—dancing around in your bare feet like a bunch of idiots?"

"I saw you there." Meg spoke up stubbornly, remembering the weird scene. "And I saw you making a spell with incense and hair, Miss Bell. Kerry and I found your book of black magic, too—the night Mrs. Stoner forgot to lock the storeroom door," she added, deciding to tell the whole truth.

"It was full of horrible, evil things," said Kerry accusingly.

"Oh, that!" Miss Bell gave a nervous little laugh. "Mrs. Stoner was Keeper of the Book in our club," she explained. "Her robe was stored in a chest at my house. I suppose the book was in the box. You saw me bring it to her, Meg."

The woman hesitated, then looked around at her "sisters." "I guess we'd better explain the whole thing," she said unhappily.

"You'd better do just that," said Uncle Hal. Meg saw that he was beginning to lose patience.

It was a strange story. "It all began when we were girls," said a slender, pretty woman who had not spoken before. "We were all in the same boarding school in Boston. Like many girls that age, we wanted to start a secret club, and—"

"Amy found that book herself, in her father's library," Mrs. Heebles broke in again, pointing to the slender woman. "We got so excited reading all about black magic that we decided to have our own witches' club. There were just thirteen of us, so it made a perfect coven. We gave ourselves odd names and even wrote them in blood. Mine was Cassandra." Her plump face turned pink with embarrassment.

Someone else took up the story. "We knew our black-magic club was all silly nonsense," she said, "but we had a lot of fun with our spooky tricks. We were all good friends, so when we left the school, we decided to have a reunion now and then and play the game just for— I don't know. Maybe we thought we'd feel young again. Anyway, we didn't think it was any sillier than men's secret lodges, where they get all done up in exotic costumes and call each other 'Grand High Whosis'!

"We met in different towns and went through the same mumbo jumbo we had learned when we were girls—and we even swore each other to secrecy."

"Not even our families ever suspected," said Cora Bell's sister.

Officer Sykes had been pacing about the room, listening in disgust. He was about to speak, when Meg stepped forward.

"You're wrong about that," she said to the last speaker. "Your own little daughter, Lisa, saw the witches at the cave. She was too frightened to talk about it."

"Oh, the poor little thing," whimpered Mrs. Heebles.

"I suppose you all thought your club was harmless," said Uncle Hal. "I hope you see now that even playing at witchcraft can be dangerous."

"Well, if *they* didn't send these letters," said Officer Sykes, slapping them against his palm, "then who did? And why? Looks as if we're right back where we started."

That was a sobering thought. Meg was more than happy that Betsy's mother and her friends were not guilty of vicious activities, but the mystery of Emily's persecution remained to be solved.

As the group broke up and drifted toward the hall, Meg heard Officer Sykes's final warning.

"As for you good ladies," he said sourly. "I advise you to have a burning. Get rid of those lunatic black robes and act like sensible grown women!"

14
WHO? WHO? WHO?

"They weren't really witches, after all."

Meg and Kerry were back in their room. Kerry was at the window, her elbows on the sill. There was a discouraged look on her freckled face, and she sounded almost disappointed at the way things had turned out.

"Of course they weren't," said Meg impatiently. She was lying on the bed. "We should have known all along that it was just a silly game. But, secret or not, somebody in this town knows about the witches' club. Somebody used those black-magic tricks as a cover-up, to scare Emily into leaving."

Meg knew now that she and Kerry had been so sure of the witches' guilt that they had failed to consider other clues to the mystery. She also knew that there *were* other clues. They were filed somewhere deep in her mind, and she couldn't drag them out.

She stared despairingly at the ceiling wallpaper. The quaint yellow figures danced before her eyes. Who had the chance to send those letters from out of town? Who could have stolen the rag doll from the Stoner house and the black-magic stones from Uncle Hal's cabin? Who was able to go anywhere in town without attracting suspicion?

Suddenly Kerry spoke again. "There go Dr. Willoughby and his nurse," she said. "Miss Armstrong is driving, and they're in an awful hurry. Someone must be sick—"

Meg sat bolt upright, no longer listening. Something had popped into her mind. With a painful click, her memory had awakened.

"Kerry," she cried, "is Officer Sykes's car still outside? I want to ask him something."

Kerry leaned farther out of the window. "Yes," she said. "He's standing beside it, talking to your uncle."

Meg bounded from the bed.

"What's it all about?" demanded Kerry.

But Meg was already out of the room and halfway down the first flight of stairs. Kerry followed.

Uncle Hal and the officer were deep in a serious conversation. They paused and looked up when dark-haired Meg came flying toward them.

"Officer Sykes," Meg asked breathlessly, "do you

118

know if Dr. Willoughby was in Merrybones fifteen years ago?''

The old man frowned. He was plainly surprised by the question, as was Uncle Hal. "Well, I can't say for sure, Meg," Sykes replied. "I doubt it, though. Doc started his practice here about ten years ago."

"What are you driving at, Meg?" Uncle Hal asked.

"I think he *was* in Merrybones long before," Meg declared. Quickly she told them about the odd incident in the boat. She was looking toward the hotel at the end of town, and she had a sudden inspiration as she finished explaining.

"If he was here," she said, "he might have stayed at the hotel, Mr. Sykes. Would there be a record?"

The man pursed his lips thoughtfully. "I suppose there is. It's a law that hotels have to keep records of people who register. I don't know for how long, though. But now that you mention it, Meg, I do seem to recall somebody coming to town and asking questions about the Hawthorne family—but I sure never connected it with the doc. Anyway," he added, "Emily's father died twenty years ago."

Uncle Hal was very much disturbed. "I think you're barking up the wrong tree, Meg, if you're suspecting Fred Willoughby. But since you raised the question, we'd better check it out."

119

Mr. Sykes heaved a sigh. "It'll be a job, going through those old books, Mr. Ashley. But you're right —let's get to it." He opened the car door.

"Could you drop us at Emily's house?" Kerry asked. "Since the witches' club didn't write those awful letters, whoever did might make more trouble. We'd better go see how she is."

"A good idea," said Uncle Hal.

Meg quickly agreed. She had been more anxious than ever about their new friend. So far, they had really been no help at all to Emily.

"You stay here," said her uncle as the girls got out of the car at Emily's gate. "I'll come by later." The car wheeled around and headed toward the hotel.

To their dismay, the girls found Emily gone. Clyde Stoner was there, packing books and dishes and looking pretty glum.

"Miss Hawthorne called me real early this morning to ask if I could help her," he said. "She's made up her mind to resign from the school and go back to her aunt's place. She said she doesn't want to stay where she isn't wanted. I told her the kids all liked her—"

"Where is Emily now?" asked Meg.

"She got a call on the telephone. I answered it first. It was somebody with a high, funny voice—like it

120

was faked. I got Miss Hawthorne, and she listened and got all excited. She said somebody had her cat locked up. They said if she'd come right away, she could get it.''

"Why didn't you go with her?" asked Kerry furiously. "It might be a trap. Where did she go?"

"I don't know," the boy retorted. "And I did offer to go, but she said she had to be alone. She lit out in that little old car of hers. I guess that witch gang is finally getting their way.''

"It wasn't the witch gang, Clyde," Meg said flatly. "It's somebody else, and I just wish we knew who." She paced back and forth a few times, muttering impatiently about having to just wait around instead of doing something about Emily. "Come on, Kerry," she said finally. "We might as well help Clyde."

Unhappily, as they awaited Uncle Hal's return, they set about wrapping Emily's pretty china to put in boxes. They told Clyde about the morning's events at the big house. He was so astonished when they told him that his mother had been a member of the black-magic club for twenty years that he sat down on a stool and let them do all the work.

"You were right, Meg!" Officer Sykes looked at Meg with new respect when he and Hal returned from their search. "Doc Willoughby was in Merrybones long before he came here to practice. He stayed two days. I wonder why he never mentioned it. . . ."

"Let's go ask him," suggested Meg's uncle.

"He might not be in his office," said Kerry. "I saw him and his nurse driving off somewhere a while ago."

He was not in his office, but his nurse, Della Armstrong, was there. She had been weeping, and her faded blue eyes were rimmed with red.

The waiting room was in disorder, and, glaring at Officer Sykes, Nurse Armstrong snapped, "He's gone, and he isn't coming back!"

Officer Sykes glared back at the woman and asked, unbelievingly, "You mean he's gone for good—moved *away?*"

"That's right," she told him bitterly. "And it's all because of *her.*"

Della didn't have to explain who *her* was. Somehow Meg knew at once that she referred to Emily. Because of Emily, Dr. Willoughby was fleeing from Merrybones . . . and Meg was beginning to suspect why.

"Are you sure he's left town?" Hal asked quietly over the officer's shoulder.

"I drove him to the plane myself. He had to get it

123

fueled up and told me to come back here to look after the office. He—he gave me his car," she added. "He was so good. . . . He didn't want to leave the town without a doctor; he took two trips to Boston last week to persuade some young man to come and take over his practice.

"Dr. White is coming in the morning, but I'll never work for *him*," she went on. The tears again spilled over her face. "Dr. Willoughby saved my brother's life—" She turned and rushed from the room.

"Poor woman," said Uncle Hal softly as they left the building. "What do we do now?"

Officer Sykes set his jaw. "We're going to take a run out to the airstrip, on the chance that he hasn't left yet. I've got some questions I'd like to ask Doc Willoughby."

15

ABRACADABRA

Officer Sykes was the only lawman in Merrybones, and he was not slow in the pursuit of justice. He raised a cloud of dust on his way to the airstrip.

Nobody expected to find Dr. Willoughby still in town. But when they arrived, there sat the small white plane with the red cross on its side. Mr. Sykes looked inside and saw a pile of suitcases behind the cockpit.

Mr. Link, the tall man who managed the hangar, came out to speak with them.

"Yep, Doc was all ready to go," he said. "He seemed mighty impatient to leave. Then Mr. Wiley came driving up. That baby of his was awful sick again. You know Doc Willoughby; he just grabbed his bag and went."

"We'll wait right here for him," said Officer Sykes stubbornly. "If he's so all-fired anxious to leave, he'll be back."

He was right. Within half an hour, Dr. Willoughby was delivered back to his plane by Mr. Wiley. He got out of his car, carrying his black bag, and came slowly toward the plane.

"Doc"—Officer Sykes wasted no time in getting to the point—"I believe you have some explaining to do."

Dr. Willoughby looked questioningly at Hal and the girls. "I'm sorry, Mr. Sykes, but I have an appointment in Boston—"

"Appointment or no appointment—I won't waste words, Doc. When you came here to practice doctoring, you told me it was the first time you'd ever seen our little town. We just got through looking at the old hotel records. I think you forgot another little visit, Doc—about fifteen years ago."

For a moment the man stood rigidly silent. Then he nodded. "Yes, I did spend a couple of days here— right after I graduated from college."

"And maybe that wasn't your first visit," Sykes persisted. "Could it be you were here when Miss Emily Hawthorne was a little girl? Could you be the man who phoned me that night when her father took sick?"

Meg was watching the doctor's face. She saw it whiten and the haggard lines deepen.

126

"Could we go back to my office and talk this over?" He sounded terribly weary. "It's a rather long story, but I suppose it must be told."

"I don't believe he did it," Kerry whispered staunchly in Meg's ear when they were in the car again. "He's so good to everybody."

Meg didn't answer, but there was a slight lump in her own throat. She was a little frightened at where all her bright ideas were leading them.

Della Armstrong was not in sight when they arrived back at the doctor's office. "You'd better stay in the waiting room," said Uncle Hal in a low voice to Meg and Kerry as Dr. Willoughby opened the door to his private office.

The doctor heard him. "No, Hal," he said. "Let them come in, too. I know they love Emily and have been trying to help her. They deserve to hear what I have to say."

He sat behind his desk, fingering the only thing left on it—a glass paperweight.

"You guessed right, Mr. Sykes," he said in his low, gentle voice. "I *was* in Merrybones almost twenty years ago, and I happened to be in the woods the night Emily's father took sick. I found him on the ground and tried to revive him. When I couldn't, I looked in his wallet to see who he was—"

127

"And you found the money, didn't you, Doc?" Sykes asked. "Several thousand dollars?"

The gray eyes never wavered. "Yes," he said shortly. "It seemed to me like a gift from heaven. I was just seventeen, and all my life I had wanted to become a doctor. You see, I had come up here to get a job in the lumber mills so I could earn the money to enter college. Unfortunately, I found the mills closed down.

"I had an old wreck of a car, but I didn't even have money for food. So I took that man's money, and I ran away. I did call, though, and tell you where to find the man." He paused for a long moment. "The very next day I regretted having taken the money. I made up my mind to come back and return it—"

"But you read the paper, didn't you?" said Sykes. Now he was like a relentless terrier, with his prey cornered. "You learned that Hawthorne had a little girl with him that night, who might have seen you steal that money."

"Yes, and I thought I would be blamed for the man's death, too," the doctor said heavily. "I knew if that happened, I'd never become a doctor. So I kept the money. I entered premed school, and everything went great for me. I got scholarships and summer jobs, and I was finally able to replace every cent

I stole—in a bank account for that little girl.

"When I finished college, I came back here. I meant to return the money, but the child was gone. She had gone to live with an aunt somewhere. You may not believe it," he added, "but I tried for years to locate her. To ease my conscience, I began writing all this down in a diary."

The little blue book! thought Meg.

"When I finally finished my medical training, I came straight to Merrybones," he said softly. "I decided to devote my life to this community. I learned to love the place and the people—"

"Then Emily Hawthorne came back!" Meg didn't realize that she had said the words aloud.

"Yes, Meg. And every time I looked at her, it was like a stab in the heart. The money I had stolen belonged to her, yet if I confessed and returned it, my work here would be finished. If I could only get her out of town, I could send her the money—anonymously. I tried to persuade her to move away, but she wouldn't go—"

"So you decided to force her to leave." Mr. Sykes pulled the two poison-pen letters from his pocket. He held them out to the doctor. "Recognize these, Doc?"

"No!" The word burst from Meg's lips. It was a small explosion of protest. "Dr. Willoughby didn't

write those horrible letters!''

While she was listening to the doctor, Meg had been absently staring at the door. It was slightly ajar. She had seen a swish of white skirts and the back of a hand—a woman's rough-skinned hand, with several fresh scratches. And suddenly—*abracadabra*—just like that, the truth came to her!

There was only one person in Merrybones who could have written those letters.

16
THE BLUEBERRY BASH

Meg jumped to her feet and dashed into the waiting room. The white-clad figure was fleeing toward the door. Meg caught up with her and grabbed her by the arm.

"Wait, please, Miss Armstrong," she begged. Her voice was almost gentle. "I think Officer Sykes would like to ask you a few questions, too."

By now Uncle Hal and the others were behind her. Meg turned, still gripping the nurse's arm, to find them staring at her in amazement.

"What's the meaning of this, Meg?" her uncle demanded sternly.

Della Armstrong shook herself free. She stood stubbornly straight against the door, her weather-beaten face contorted with emotion.

"Never mind, Mr. Ashley. *I* did it. *I* wrote the letters," she said. Her eyes flashed. "When that young teacher came to town—that Emily Hawthorne—I knew everything would be spoiled. I knew that unless I could scare her away, the doctor's life would be ruined, and so would mine.

"He made one mistake," she cried. *"One* mistake, when he was just a boy. And he paid for it a thousand times! No one in town knew the truth, except me. I —I found out—" Her face reddened.

"It's all right, Della." The doctor went to her and took her kindly by the arm. "The truth is out, and I'm glad. I suspected that you had found my diary. You did read it, didn't you?"

She nodded her gray head. "Yes. When you left me alone here, I'd get it out of your desk. I knew all about the money, and I knew you were planning to leave Merrybones and get some young doctor to take your place. I didn't want you to go. This town needs you. So I wrote the letters. Vacationers who came in private planes mailed them for me from Boston.

"I thought I could scare Miss Hawthorne away," she said. Her shoulders drooped. "I never intended to hurt her. . . ."

"But you did hurt her, Miss Armstrong," said Uncle Hal. "When she found that doll in her cupboard yesterday, she was terrified. She might have been seriously injured."

"And how did you know about the witches' club, anyway?" asked Kerry, her blue eyes big. "They said it was a secret."

Della laughed—a strange, harsh sound. "A nurse learns a lot of things she never tells," she said. "One of the women was sick once. She had a high fever, and she muttered and mumbled all about those meetings and the black-magic spells.

"When I was in Mr. Ashley's cabin—that day I first met you girls—I saw those gray rocks. I went back when he was gone—"

"And you took Betsy Stoner's doll when Kim Millard was sick," Kerry interrupted. "Betsy and I looked all over for it."

"And how about Emily's cat?" asked Meg. She looked pointedly at the scratches on the woman's hand. "You took Melissa both times."

"Yes. That cat always spit and fought when I tried to touch it, but I knew it was the thing the schoolteacher loved most."

"Where is the animal now?" Mr. Sykes had been standing in the background, listening with some chagrin as the drama unfolded. He now moved up to confront the nurse. "I hope you haven't gone so far as to hurt Miss Hawthorne's pet."

Just then, as if in answer to his question, the door

opened, and in came Emily herself. She was smiling, and in her arms was the big black cat with the green eyes.

"I saw the car outside," she said to Meg's uncle. "I hoped I'd find you all here."

The mysterious caller, who was Della, of course, had been true to her word. When she had discovered that her plan had failed and the doctor was leaving, she had called to tell Emily where the cat was hidden. Emily had found Melissa in an abandoned shed outside of town.

"What will happen to them now?" Meg asked a little later, as she and Kerry walked back to the Stoner house with Uncle Hal.

"I don't think we have to worry," he said. "Emily said she'll refuse to press charges, and Officer Sykes appeared to be satisfied with her decision."

"I feel sorry for Miss Armstrong," said Meg.

"Yes, the poor woman. She's been working too hard. Out of loyalty to Fred Willoughby, she became reckless. As for the doctor, Meg, he's making full restitution to Emily for the wrong he did years ago. He was very young when he stole that money. I'm sure that nobody concerned is anxious to discuss either him or Della Armstrong with the rest of the town. Merrybones likes and *needs* both of them, and what's past is past, right?"

At that, Kerry nudged Meg. "How did you guess that it was the nurse, after all?" she asked.

Meg smiled. "It was those scratches, Kerry. I saw scratches on her arms the first day we met her, but I didn't think about them. Then yesterday, in the doctor's waiting room, when she was reading the diary, she hid her hands from me. The scratches were new, and they looked just like the ones my Thunder gave a mean boy back in Hidden Springs. He was pulling Thunder's tail—remember?"

Kerry laughed. "We'll have to give Melissa credit for helping to solve the mystery," she said. "She left her own clues."

"Well, it's all over now," said Meg happily, "and I'm glad. I'm tired of chasing witches."

Uncle Hal smiled. "So am I," he agreed. "I'm going to go up to the cabin and loll around and do a little painting. Why don't you two find Betsy and go and have a little fun? Before you know it, our vacation will be over."

In the next few days, Meg and Kerry made up for lost time. They spent hours riding. They fished in the lake. They took another trip to Blueberry Ridge to pick fruit for Mrs. Stoner. This time Uncle Hal went along.

Soon after that, Meg awoke to the heavenly smell of deep-dish blueberry pie. It was the day of the Blueberry Bash.

Almost everyone in Merrybones attended the celebration, except Dr. Willoughby and Della Armstrong, who were happily back at their work and out in the country, waiting for a reluctant baby to be born.

There was community singing, and there was square dancing. There were blueberry pies and blueberry dumplings and blueberry duff. There were blueberry puddings and blueberry cakes and even homemade blueberry ice cream. The good cooks of the town had done themselves proud.

Even the thirteen witches came. They were in ordinary clothes, however, having made a solemn vow never to practice their black arts again—though they would continue to hold their reunions.

But of all the guests present, the most popular was Miss Emily Hawthorne. Everyone had heard of her decision to stay in Merrybones, and everyone came up to tell her how much the town appreciated it.

Uncle Hal filched some roses from Mrs. Stoner's garden and teasingly crowned Emily Queen of the Blueberry Bash.

"It's the best vacation ever," said Kerry, mumbling the words around a huge bite of blueberry pie.

Meg agreed with her. More important, something miraculous had happened to Merrybones, Maine. Everyone seemed suddenly kinder to everyone else. Meg looked around with wondering eyes. Could it be witchcraft?

Then the answer came to her. The magic was love!

YOU WILL ENJOY

THE TRIXIE BELDEN SERIES

31 Exciting Titles

TRIXIE BELDEN MYSTERY-QUIZ BOOKS

2 Fun-Filled Volumes

THE MEG MYSTERIES

6 Baffling Adventures

ALSO AVAILABLE

Algonquin
Alice in Wonderland
A Batch of the Best
More of the Best
Still More of the Best
Black Beauty
The Call of the Wild
Dr. Jekyll and Mr. Hyde
Frankenstein
Golden Prize
Gypsy from Nowhere
Gypsy and Nimblefoot
Gypsy and the Moonstone Stallion
Lassie—Lost in the Snow
Lassie—The Mystery of Bristlecone Pine
Lassie—The Secret of the Smelters' Cave
Lassie—Trouble at Panter's Lake
Match Point
Seven Great Detective Stories
Sherlock Holmes
Shudders
Tales of Time and Space
Tee-Bo and the Persnickety Prowler
Tee-Bo in the Great Hort Hunt
That's Our Cleo
The War of the Worlds
The Wonderful Wizard of Oz